Eatin

Eating Between the Lines

Kevin Major

Doubleday Canada Limited

Canadian Cataloguing in Publication Data
    Major, Kevin, 1949-
        Eating between the lines

ISBN 0-385-25293-5

I. Title

PS 8576.A5E3 1991 JC813'.54 C91-094133-5
PZ7.M34Ea 1991

Cover design by Tania Craan
Illustration by Marion Stuck
Printed and bound in the USA
Published in Canada by
Doubleday Canada Limited
105 Bond Street
Toronto, Ontario
M5B 1Y3

For Luke

ONE

Jackson flew back from New York knowing that he would forever love the combination of an overstuffed pastrami sandwich and blueberry cheesecake, and that he was going to be an artist. The Big Apple had done it for him, given him a taste of just what he thought he'd been looking for in this life. He was barely airborne before he was dying to go back again.

He had loved it all, even the stink of exhaust fumes mixed with the reek from the gutters and the smoke from the hot dog and pretzel stands. It was all he could do to keep from bursting out in song from the Broadway show they had seen. He rubbed his fingers lovingly over the face of the Rolex watch he had picked up dirt-cheap in Times Square, as he took one last lingering look down at the soaring peaks of Manhattan.

"Know what I really love about it?" he said to his mother. "There is nothing it hasn't got — the filthy rich, the filthy poor, the half-decently sensible, the crazies — all squat together on 22 square miles. Every kind of race and religion you can think of, and music and art and basketball. And *food*. Man, what food."

"We'll be back," his mother promised, leaning over and peering with him through the Air Canada window. She was wearing the classy outfit she had found in a discount store in SoHo that sold only black designer clothes, with the labels missing. The store was called Short and Black and to the Point.

"You're darn right we'll be back. I'd say mid-winter break, Kath." He shortened her name at times when she particularly meant a lot to him. And this was definitely one of those times, he thought. He had never felt as close to his mother as he had on this trip.

"Your father won't think much of that."

"We'll work on him. Get him to come too. Twist his arm. Bribe him. Torture him."

"The torture that would get your father to New York hasn't been invented yet."

The torture started the minute they emerged from Customs. Jackson spotted his father. He snapped himself out of his slug-like depression and burst into a wild lament about all the things his father had missed by not going with them — the unbelievable amount of stuff that came free in the hotel bathroom, all the bargains in camera equipment and computer software and check shirts with button-down collars. Jackson flashed him a look at his watch.

After he heard how much it cost, his father grimaced. "It's got to be fake."

"That's what I like about it! Who can tell the difference? And who cares if they do? Great, eh?"

His father shook his head. His mother told Jackson to cool it. And he shut up after a while when he saw that his father was only going to again dismiss whatever he said as the obscure workings of a teenage mind. It had been a good try at least. And there were other ways of tackling it. He made a rough list in his head in the back seat of the Volvo during the drive home.

Jackson couldn't see that he was in any way a disagreeable sort of teenager. He smiled a lot. He didn't come home in agony about the way life was treating him. He didn't hate his parents. He was kind, considerate, generous. He had been a Boy Scout when he was younger, and he still had all his badges in a Ziploc bag in the top drawer of his dresser. He didn't show up late at night foggy with drugs or with liquor on his breath, and he didn't spend endless hours listening to loud music that made girls out to be sex objects. He knew for sure he was heterosexual. He could have gone on and on. He couldn't see what else his father wanted him to be.

His father said he talked too much. Jackson was pretty sure his father loved him a lot, and he did seem cautiously proud that Jackson had so much self-confidence. And his father had to be thankful that there was none of that snarly rebellion he must have heard about from other people who had teenage sons. He had nothing against the way Jackson dressed or what he did to his hair. He just said he talked too much.

His mother didn't mind even that. She said it showed a way with words that was bound to serve him well no matter what he did with his life. Of course it had to be a welcome contrast to the pecking of computer keys or the unbiased opinions of "The Nightly Business Report" that told her that her husband was somewhere in the house.

"It shows the artist in him," Jackson overheard her saying to his father one night, about a week after the trip to New York, when he happened by the partially opened door to their bedroom.

He heard no answer from his father, only the click of his

bedside lamp, leaving his mother to go back to whatever she had been doing.

An hour later she came downstairs, where Jackson had gone to watch Monty Python's *The Meaning of Life*, yet again. She sat on the edge of the couch with a glass of a bubbling antacid. She had come in at the part where the guy explodes from having eaten so much. They had the biggest kind of laugh together — a great relief for them both.

"How have you been feeling since we got back?" she asked him during a part she found too gross to watch. He should have known he hadn't been doing much of a job of hiding his boredom.

"Everything here is so dull and predictable. It makes it damned hard for anyone growing up to be an artist."

"They don't call this place the curling capital of Canada for nothing."

"No excitement at the gallery?"

"Nobody is interested in anything if it doesn't match their drapes and sofas."

"Bor-ing."

"What you need is a girlfriend."

He smiled. Could anyone have a more understanding parent?

The fizz had gone from what was left in her glass. She kissed him good night and walked up the stairs, leaving Jackson with a new and even deeper appreciation of his mother.

He wished he could have had a similar encounter with his father. Not that Jackson wasn't reasonably happy to be his son, especially when he saw what fate had dealt some others he knew. It was just that — well — his father he didn't quite understand. He couldn't get keyed up when it came time to get him a Father's Day card or save to buy him a birthday present. He tended to look at their relationship as a challenge more than anything. He fantasized how one day his father would throw off his preoccupation with the value of money, burn his *Consumer Reports* magazines, junk his telephoto lenses, and start doing mindless, insignificant things with his spare time.

Lately Jackson had taken to playing tricks with the order of his father's life. Like adding white sugar to his box of cereal and seeing how much more of it he would eat. And setting up the car stereo so that his father got a blast of Boxcar Willie when he turned the key on Monday morning. Little things like that, just enough to reassure himself that his father was human.

Not to his amazement, his father wrote off to the cereal company when he got to the bottom of the box and discovered what was undoubtedly sugar crystals. Even when they sent enough coupons for a case of Multi-Grain Nutri Flakes as an apology, his father was not satisfied. By then he had sworn himself onto All-Natural Cream of Oats 'n Bran, even though he had to get up ten minutes earlier each morning to cook it.

As for Boxcar Willie, Jackson found the cassette the next day in the glove compartment, neatly and permanently sealed inside its case with epoxy glue.

He had learned to live with his father, and his father with him. Unfortunately, that arrangement would not get him back to New York in anything less than a year, the time span his father told him was practical and reasonable. He'd have to wait it out like his mother suggested, or come up with a more ingenious scheme to change his father's way of looking at the world.

"Life sure is a funny thing," Jackson said to him one morning as they ate bowls of steaming All-Natural Cream of Oats 'n Bran. "One day you're here, the next day you're in the morgue, struck by a car, or choked up with some disease they got no cure for."

His father looked up from the pages of *The Microwave Food Industry Journal.* "Are you sick?" he asked.

"Not yet."

His father looked down again.

"I could be. You never know."

"You're not, Jackson, take my word for it. Eat your cereal."

Jackson coughed. His father looked at him suspiciously. "Quit faking."

"Faking today, dead tomorrow."

"Get serious."

It was not in Jackson's nature to get serious. His father knew that, but he always said it anyway. It usually meant he didn't want to talk about whatever it was he wasn't talking about.

"Get serious?" Jackson questioned. "I am serious."

His father ignored him. Jackson took a second helping of All-Natural Cream of Oats 'n Bran.

His father looked up again. He stared at him. "Bowel trouble?" he asked.

"Nothing serious . . . I guess."

He glared at Jackson with genuine concern.

"I get like that when I stay in one place too long. Doctors have a term for it — stationary constipation."

His father's look turned sour. "Crap."

"Easier said than done."

Jackson lost him to the magazine once again.

Jackson came to admit that it did sound useless. Was there no way the guy was going to crack, no matter how strong or how brilliant the pressure? What was needed was a jolt powerful enough that it would rearrange his father's gray matter.

"Remember when you were my age?"

"I certainly do."

"Well?"

"That's the point." His father paused. "If I knew then what I know now I wouldn't have been so damn wild."

"Wild?" The idea left Jackson spellbound.

"Before I left Newfoundland I wasted years, Jackson, years. Roaming from job to job, listening to Cat Stevens records, steeping myself in the so-called wisdom of the East, looking for answers, thinking I'd found them, only to realize in the end that I was going nowhere. Meanwhile, the guys here were getting the real jobs. And now, you know what they are? They're the presidents of the companies, and I'm still slogging away, the johnny-come-lately, waiting for the next promotion."

"But are they happy?"

"Is that really relevant? What is happiness?"

"A good question."

"And how will I ever know if they are or if they're not, if I don't get there to find out?"

"Right."

Jackson was left to flounder in his doubts about what had just passed between them. One thing for sure — there was a lot more to account for his father's state of mind than he had ever realized before. No longer would Jackson be able to think of him as merely an obstacle to getting back to New York. Behind that *Microwave Food Industry Journal* there was a lot of human suffering.

For now, Jackson had to resign himself to living on memories of the trip.

Since his return he had peppered the wall next to his bed with dozens of reminders of the good time he'd had — snapshots, postcards, brochures, ticket stubs, a floor plan from Bloomingdale's, a dried leaf from Central Park, a napkin from the Carnegie Deli that he was sure still smelled of the pastrami and cheesecake.

And on the wall opposite his bed he had pinned the poster his mother had bought for him at the Metropolitan Museum of Art — a picture by Gauguin of two bare-breasted girls on a beach, somewhere, it didn't exactly matter where. He was surprised at the time that he could convince his mother to buy it for him. He thought maybe it was her way of encouraging his interest in art. Or, more likely, compensation for following her for six hours through the museum. Whatever the reason, it definitely made the view from his bed a much more interesting one than it had been with the poster of a wrinkled dog wearing sunglasses.

Actually he had loved the six hours in the museum. He hadn't thought the building would be so massive and there could be so much to see. He thought it was going to be just painting and sculpture and people pretending to understand them. In fact, at times he was almost struck dumb by what he saw. It sent him back into worlds he had only ever studied in textbooks. It was like, if there hadn't been that class from the girls' school to follow, he could have lost himself in it all. He pictured himself a Roman, a knight in medieval Europe, a Japanese artisan. Gauguin among the girls.

The gold he had seen in some of the collections had particularly fascinated him. In part it was because he had known very little real gold in his life. For some reason his father had a great aversion to it. As a consequence, his mother hesitated to buy any gold jewelry and tended toward sterling silver. Even her taste for that had started to draw his father's eyebrows together in contradicting ways.

His father's only concession to the unmentionable element was the gold edges of the leather-bound books he bought. For several years now he had been a member of Classics, a book club that to date had filled the oak bookcase in the living room with close to a hundred expensive editions of what it called "the greatest literary works of all time." They stood in line beautifully, varying with good taste in thickness and height and the color of the leather. His father loved to look at them as he passed by after supper on his way to his favorite spot for reading the evening paper. Occasionally he would take one down and stare at it with pleasure for a long time, and return it to its place, still pleased with himself.

It was seen as his father's weakness, this book club. Neither Jackson nor his mother ever questioned the fact that they had never seen him read even one of the books cover to cover. That seemed to be beside the point. He would pore over the monthly brochure from the book club for what seemed like hours. Jackson figured that his father had some pattern to the arrangement of the books in the bookcase, and that the decision of what to order depended a lot on how well a book could fit that pattern. He had tested his theory by switching the positions of two of the books. His father picked it up in no time, and blamed the change on his wife.

Indeed, Katherine was the only one who ever disturbed the sacred lineup in order to actually read one of the books. Even then she knew it was expected that the book be back exactly in its place when she wasn't in the physical process of reading it. She had even been known to start one of the books and then buy a paperback copy so she could finish the story in comfort.

When they thought about it, Jackson and his mother knew that this obsession with order of books in a bookcase was odd. They no longer thought about it. Except occasionally his mother would say, "It could be worse. It could be Salvador Dali prints. Or Robert Bateman."

Jackson didn't need convincing. He had listened to that

line of reasoning for years, ever since his mother had begun work at the Jonathan Walker Gallery. What started out as a love of art quickly turned to a passion, until it filled her life. Hence the trip to New York, and hence the bare breasts on Jackson's wall.

And hence, too, Jackson's name. He started life as plain Jack, that is, a variation on his father's name, John. (JFK had been a hero to both his parents, especially his mother, whose birth father was an American G.I. named Hank stationed briefly in Newfoundland after the Second World War.) But as the distance between father and son grew and the shine went off the Kennedy years, Katherine began toying with the idea of changing her son's name in some way. They had moved that summer and she had just started her first job at an art gallery, so come September he went to kindergarten as Jackson. Like Jackson Pollock, the painter, his mother said and showed him some reproductions from art books. Like Jackson Browne, the singer, his mother tried again and played him "Running on Empty."

Jackson thought it was neat, and explained it all to his kindergarten teacher, who made long notes for the school files. John thought it fine too, not showing a great deal of concern about it, being so caught up in his new job as a microwavable food product analyst. The family weathered the reluctance of relatives to accept the change of name, and then Michael Jackson released "Thriller" and in quick succession became number one in the universe, did more weird things to his face, started sleeping in an oxygen chamber, and offered one million dollars for the skeleton of the Elephant Man.

"One day," his mother tried to console him, "Jesse Jackson will be president of the United States."

He learned to live with it. Just as he learned to live with the other quirks of his existence. And as he grew into a teenager he came to appreciate that there was a distinctive history to his name and that he wasn't the butt of "jack off" jokes as was the one person in the school who bore his former name.

And as he grew into a teenager there were also a lot more important things crowding his mind, of course. Girls, and their lack of prominence in his life. School, and its relevance to him as a probable doctor, then talk-show host, and now artist. Rock and roll and basketball. Girls, and what they thought about the way he dressed and cut his hair.

It was for these very reasons that he had not noticed that his parents were talking to each other even less than they had been the year before. It struck him only when he showed up unexpectedly in the back room of the art gallery one Saturday afternoon after the trip to New York and saw his mother with her arm around the waist of one of the gallery artists and his hand resting on her shoulder. It seemed an odd way to be admiring the painting of a dead moose.

The way they separated when they saw him was the giveaway. Not suddenly, to make him think for sure they were doing something wrong. But slowly, then jokingly, asking him what he thought of the painting.

Jackson shrugged. "Different."

"That all?"

"Life-like, disturbing."

He could see her start to squirm.

"Upsetting. Confusing."

"Lifeless," she said. "Try that."

Now he was even more confused. Was there really something going on between her and that guy or was it just a way of looking at things she had picked up in New York? He didn't want to overreact and risk not looking cool about it all.

He didn't ask to borrow the car as he had come to do. Instead he made some lame excuse about needing money and then turned to leave when she gave it to him. She asked him if he wouldn't stay and see more of the work of this new artist whose show they were hanging the following week. He said no, and left her wondering if his coolness was a reaction to her or to the moose.

And that was just the way he wanted it. He forgot about picking up his friends and driving around, and instead walked all the way back home. It gave him plenty of time to consider the possibilities. Either it was for real, this hanging on to each other, or it wasn't. If it was (and he was starting to think it had to be), then he'd have to admit his father was probably what brought on the situation.

His mother seemed to be so resigned to his father's ways that the thought had never occurred to Jackson before that anything could be really off track in their marriage. They never argued. They didn't say anything that upset the other. They hardly ever talked about what was going on between them, in fact.

Near the end of his walk home, it hit Jackson like a brick wall. He, who had always been so keen on conversation, should have known better. This lack of communication between his parents was not a good thing.

He realized that there had been a time when they did talk more. They made plans together. And they talked about their younger days, when they were teenagers. He even remembered them laughing together at the pictures of his mother in flowered bell bottoms and his father with a ponytail. She said she was madly in love with Paul McCartney and he said he was probably the first one in Newfoundland ever to try tie-dying. They told him how they were married at sunrise on a hill in St. John's that overlooked salt water and how all the people there joined hands in a circle around them and sang "Come Together."

Jackson had problems imagining it all. If it was true, then what had happened to bring about this parting of ways? Maybe he was the one to blame. Maybe his failure to live up to some expectation or other had forced them apart.

No, he refused to accept any of the blame for it. It was a fact of life that people grow apart sometimes instead of together like they vowed to do. You have to learn to accept the good with the bad. The ups with the downs.

It all sounded so rational. So sickly rational, in fact, that it drove him near depression. But he snapped himself out of it, and by the time his mother showed up in his bedroom later, he felt perfectly all right, positive that no matter what she might say, he could keep a handle on his emotions.

"The poster looks great," she said. "Gauguin has always been one of my favorites."

"So real you want to stroke it," he commented, echoing what she always said about wildlife artists whose work she didn't like.

She must have sensed his mood and decided it better to get right to the point. "It's not what you're thinking."

"Huh!"

Suddenly she didn't seem so sure of herself. "We're only friends."

"I wasn't born yesterday, Katherine," he said, neither impressed nor amused.

It was obviously proving more difficult than she had prepared herself for. He picked up the conversation when the silence became unbearably long. "Let's just get some things straight."

And here he hesitated a few seconds for effect. She sat down quietly on the edge of the bed.

"I realize that Dad hasn't exactly been a ball of fire these last few years and maybe there are lots of reasons to look for a little spark in your life somewhere else, but that doesn't give you the right to shut me off in the dark and let me believe everything's the same as it's always been. I'm part of this family too and I like to think that my feelings are just as important as everybody else's. It might not always look like it, but I really appreciate Dad for what he is. He might not be everything you need in a husband and he might not be everything I need in a father, but the guy's not half bad. He doesn't fool around, he's dependable, he's responsible. I'm not saying he couldn't be better. I'm not saying that. I'm not sure what I'm saying. But let's get one thing perfectly clear — it's no fun when you know you're being lied to."

The bedroom was oddly silent when he finally stopped, but he felt a whole lot better now that his frustrations were out in the open. His mother sat quietly, looking as though she'd had enough.

"Maybe," she said finally, "you're right."

He was surprised. But he wasn't about to stop at that.

"So what do we do?"

"He's not the man I married."

"So we get him back to the way he used to be. We root him out of this condition of his."

"Jackson, I'm not sure if it can be done."

He had to admit he hadn't gotten too far trying to change his father's mind about New York. But this was different, this was a family at stake here.

"There's got to be some way."

"I'll try anything."

"Does that mean you're not in love with that other guy?"

"I never was."

"Honest?"

"Honest."

He believed her. They smiled with relief and hugged each

other tightly.

"But I still think he's a great artist," she said. "I just adore his moose."

TWO

During the next several days Jackson managed to get a better grip on himself and the world around him. He set his parental problems aside after convincing his mother that what was needed was a wildly artful scheme that would rekindle the life she first had with his father. He left it to her to work out the details.

He concentrated his own energies on school and his love of the opposite sex. He felt no less anxious than he did thinking about his family, but it was a relief to be on familiar territory.

Over the past few weeks he had fallen behind in almost every one of his classes. He was known to his teachers as an intelligent individual who talked more than he worked. He considered that a fair assessment, and it didn't really bother him, in view of the work he sometimes found himself assigned to do. And in view of the many female diversions wandering about the school. But as a grade eleven student, he knew he would have to apply his talents to less interesting subjects or risk low marks, failure, and then dismissal by the very same females who kept him from concentrating on his work. It was a vicious circle, but one that he was determined to talk himself into breaking. He could be cruel on himself when he needed to be.

To a point, that was.

Sara was the girl of his dreams. She had everything he ever thought he could wish for in a girl: beauty without a touch of conceit, intelligence without a hint of arrogance, and a great way with well-fitting clothes. When she came near him, he was left speechless. That in itself was proof enough. But then there was the time she told him she liked his haircut. He had been in a trance ever since.

For years his hormones had been hinting that it was about time he had some real love-interest in his life. He had played with the idea off and on, and he had even gone out on a number of dates, with varying degrees of attachment. They came to an abrupt halt within weeks of Sara transferring to his school. No one else was even coming close to stirring up his interest in the way Sara did each and every time she passed him in the corridor. He couldn't understand it, but thought maybe it had a lot to do with the fact that, like him, she had been born in Newfoundland.

It was hard on him, really hard, especially since the school's production of *Romeo and Juliet*, in which Sara had played Juliet and Jackson had almost played Romeo. He was the understudy, but the other fellow didn't get the least bit sick or break a thing. And besides being what Jackson knew was a lousy actor, the guy was the somebody Sara called a boyfriend. His name was Adam, and if that wasn't unoriginal enough, Jackson found out he played hockey and got all A's, except for Canadian History. Jackson couldn't stand the guy. He thought seriously of taking up some martial art and having a go at him.

But he knew better than to think that Sara would respond to such primitive methods. She was a modern woman who would no doubt be disgusted if he were to force himself between them. No, it would take a more imaginative and intelligent plan to lure her away, a plan that he hadn't quite decided on but whose consequences seemed to take up a great deal of his thoughts.

It would have to start with more impressive marks in school. Not an easy job, considering the pile of assignments and exams he had facing him. He would tackle the assignments to begin, he thought, then concentrate on the exams, and then glory in the results, and then watch as her resistance to him weakened, until finally that first date and her falling hopelessly and recklessly in love with him, free of all inhibitions, wild and carefree and wanting him forever.

"Jackson."

Nothing could spoil the wonder of it all.

"Jackson, why are you staring at me like that?"

It was Sara. He came quickly to what senses he could get a hold on. He had wandered up the corridor toward the gym while waiting for the school bus, not thinking she would be at the water fountain, or wearing what she was wearing.

"Sorry. It wasn't you I was staring at. It's the wall behind you. That poster on the wall behind you."

Sara looked at the wall. The only thing there was a list of fire regulations and an emergency exit plan.

"I like to play it safe," he said. "Can't take any chances, not when things get hot, right?"

She started toward the doors to the gym, looking rather uncomfortable.

"Hey, Sara?"

She looked at him, one hand on the door.

"Know something?"

"What?"

"You look great."

She sort of rolled her eyes and blushed at the same time. It was a very confusing reaction, one that had him momentarily stuck for words.

She made a move to open the door.

"Really. I'm not just saying that for something to say."

"Why are you saying it, then?"

"Because it's something I've had on my mind for a long time. And I was thinking — why not be honest, why not say what you feel? That's what's wrong with the world — everybody's hiding their true selves. Let's face it, life is too short for that. Why not be open? Why not come right out and say it — I want to go out with you. There, so now you know. So now there's no need to play those stupid little games where I try to get you to notice me, and you play hard to get, and then I try harder, and then finally when we do go out with each other we're both sorry we hadn't done it months before. Right?"

He stood there, his hands in his jeans pockets, his shoulders shrugged, a look on his face saying: there you have it, this is who I am, I can handle whatever you throw at me.

She didn't say anything for the longest time.

It was killing him. He couldn't be this cool forever. His heart was pounding like crazy. He wouldn't be able to hold his breath much longer.

"You're forgetting one thing," she said.

He wouldn't dare try to speak. He could choke on the words. He shrugged still more.

"Compatibility."

She opened the door and disappeared inside.

He collapsed against the wall, a broad smile across his face. *Compatibility* — he'd have to look it up in the dictionary to be absolutely sure it meant everything he thought it meant. *Compatibility*. Such a wonderfully long and intelligent word. A beautiful word. One that said there was hope.

And the way he heard her say it — so calmly, so sweetly, so sensitively. Jackson glowed in the knowledge that she had not rejected him outright. There was that flicker of hope, that ray of light that he could nurture into a wild, flaming romance.

He resigned himself to the fact that it would indeed have to start with more impressive marks at school. Gone were the days when a few well-chosen words could do the trick. The only way to the heart of a girl as thoroughly modern as Sara was through her brain — a somewhat disheartening conclusion for someone as naturally conversational as Jackson, but one that he was determined to look at as a challenge. Besides, the tougher the fight, the sweeter the prize.

He wandered back through the corridor with those last words singing again and again through his head. The tougher the fight, the sweeter the prize. Was that a quote from some famous politician? It should be if it wasn't. Or had he made it up in his own moment of brilliance? Jackson, he lamented as he got aboard the bus, the country is crying out for people like you. You're wasting your time chasing girls.

He knew in his heart of hearts that he would rather be chasing girls. On the bus he made a list of all the schoolwork he had to do during the next two weeks. The list ran to ten items. By the time the bus stopped near the library, he had psyched himself up for a marathon of work. The first item on the list was an oral report on the heroic deeds of the ancient Greeks. It was due the next day.

In the library he went in search of Mrs. Landsberg. She had been helping him for years to find books for his assignments. Together they had conquered the most obscure of topics.

"Mrs. Landsberg no longer works here," he was told by someone new behind the reference desk.

"She retired?"

"Quit."

"Mrs. Landsberg?"

"So I'm told."

The new person was tall and thin and wore clunky purple jewelry. She looked to be fresh out of library school, but Jackson was thinking that she had messed up in her career choice. He was sure she would only ever direct him to the nearest computer terminal.

He slid away from the reference desk. It was tougher without Mrs. Landsberg showing up with books he would have otherwise missed. He did find several pictureless books of great wordiness that made his heart sink at the thought of reading them. But he checked them out anyway. Then he photocopied items from a number of encyclopedias, including a powerfully graphic entry from the *Time-Life Encyclopedia of Life Before America.*

He headed home. He walked in dread of the prospect of having to filter through all that material and try to come up with a ten-minute report that would get him an A. But the longer he walked, the more he was determined to tough it out. He came through the door of the house with a look of bookish determination that would have warmed the heart of even the least gullible of his teachers.

He was surprised to encounter a mother with a look of determination equal to his own. She was holding in her hands a copy of the greatest hits of José Feliciano. She hurriedly explained that she had come up with this way-out idea of re-creating the mood of her first dates with his father. It was obvious that she was going to stop at nothing in the effort to get him back to the man he used to be.

He followed her excitedly to the kitchen. She had some fishcakes frying on the stove and brown rice, cucumber and a strong garlic dressing set out on the counter. It had all the ingredients of a very inventive plan. She rushed away to get changed, leaving Jackson to wander to the ancient turntable in the living room and linger there, trying to guess which of José Feliciano's hits was the greatest.

The choice of what to play became obvious. And when his father came through the front door and heard the words "C'mon, baby, light my fire," Jackson detected a definite loosening up of his shoulders and a smile on his face of a sort Jackson had never seen there before. His father hung by the closet door, in a trance for a moment, no doubt transported back more than a couple of decades. He actually jaunted up the four steps two at a time.

When he came into the kitchen and the smells jogged his memory once again, Jackson's heart was pounding in anticipation of what he might say or do. His mother had loosened her hair so that it could fall as long and straight as possible, and she was wearing a peasant dress she had unearthed from a trunk in the basement. She looked up at him, her string of beads momentarily getting in the way of her salad-making.

He stood perfectly still and wasn't able to utter a word for what seemed like ages. Then he said, "I'm not sure what this is all about."

Katherine started to look uncomfortable. Jackson jumped in quickly.

"I'm doing this project for school — 'Lifestyles of My Parents' Era.' You know, sort of a look back at the good old days. This brings back memories, right?"

"Does it ever."

The words came out flat and lifeless, not what Jackson

had been hoping for.

"Reminds me of that apartment we . . . I used to rent. The one with the shower that always ran cold. Never could stand the place."

"John, we had lots of good times there. That's where you proposed."

"You know, I think you might be right." There was the barest hint of that same smile.

Jackson grabbed at it. "Man, it must have been fantastic. I can picture you two now. Not much money, but desperately in love. Peace. Tranquillity. One with the universe. Full of ambitions, ready to take on the world. It must have been like really something, man. Wow!"

"I worked part-time in that fish take-out place. That's why we had so much of the damn stuff."

"You didn't care, though, right?" Jackson said. "You were young. You could live on love! And you had lots of rice and you like garlic on cucumber, right?"

"Jackson, please," his mother said.

"No . . . what he's trying to say is that fishcakes bring back very powerful images for him." He turned to his father. "Don't they, Dad?"

"Don't think I could face another one of those stupid things."

His mother marched over to the stove, seized the frying pan and dumped hot fat and fishcakes into the garbage can.

"My God, Katherine, what are you doing? You know that's gone right through the garbage bag!"

She tore off her beads, threw them into the rice and ran out of the kitchen, shouting, "That's the last meal I'm cooking for you in this house! You want dinner, you cook it yourself!"

John was stunned. He struggled for words. "I can't ever remember her getting so mad. Except for the time in the apartment before we were married when the white mouse we had got loose and scratched her *Sergeant Pepper* album."

Jackson was even more stunned. He had never seen his mother show anger so openly toward his father. He didn't know whether to cheer or cry or feel sorry for someone.

"Dad!" He had a terrible time deciding what should come next.

He stared at his father, desperate to detect some change, even the smallest hint that he was in some way reconsidering the direction of his life.

His father ran his hand aimlessly down the back of his head. It was something.

"Dad, did you have to?"

"She knows I'm very sensitive about food. There was no need to threaten me like that."

Jackson shook his head and took off to his bedroom in an unmistakable show of support for his mother. And there he waited for the house to settle back to being livable again.

For a couple of hours he tried working on his report on ancient Greece. His guts ached for something more palatable. How could he be expected to concentrate on schoolwork when all he could think of were the fabulous smells that usually drifted out of the kitchen at that time of the evening? What he wouldn't give for just one serving of Breast of Chicken Terre-Neuvien. His mind wandered to the poster of Gauguin's girls, but even there he could find nothing to take his mind off his stomach for more than a few delicious seconds. It was pain of the most basic kind, and when he could stand it no longer, he sneaked out of his bedroom and tiptoed down the stairs. He caught an aroma that seemed to suggest food, and so he followed it cat-like down the hallway and peered into the kitchen.

His mother was spooning out something that had just come from the microwave, prepackaged and vaguely

Oriental. In the center of the table was a something else, Danish and thawing. They were his father's newest product lines.

Jackson sat down beside her. He could see her anger had not entirely subsided, so he tried to eat what was before him with a certain amount of relish. If it had been something homemade — hamburgers, even — he might have made it through without groaning.

"Is that all there is?"

"Complain to your father. I don't see *him* come rushing home from work to spend two hours in the kitchen! Why should I be the one?"

Jackson had unleashed something that had clearly been fermenting for years. "You know he's useless in the kitchen," he offered timidly, just so she'd get it straight who she was mad with.

"He got straight A's in cooking school, for heaven's sake! Didn't you ever think it was kind of funny that he started this slide into uselessness the same week we moved here? He's hardly lifted a finger in this kitchen since. Blames it on his job, says he gets enough of cooking at work. Don't give me that garbage!"

She was probably right, thought Jackson, but why should he be made to suffer for his father's domestic shortcomings? He looked at the food in front of him and worked up enough guts to unleash a few frustrations of his own.

"Great. So I'm expected to OD on sugar and mono-sodium glutamate for however many months it takes him to get around to cooking us a meal. Great!"

"We're in this together, remember. If I'm willing to eat this stuff, then you should be, too. This is one way to show him that we really mean business."

"Sure! He won't even eat it himself!"

"That's the point!"

"Sad."

But no way would she give in. She had her mind set on this new tactic like it was the newest, most wonderful diet on the best-seller list. It made him sick to think that she could be so callous. Didn't she realize what food means to a teenage male? Wasn't this some form of adolescent neglect?

He left the house, disgusted with what his stomach was expected to suffer for the sake of their marriage. Just what was this cholesterol and additive overkill going to prove?

He ran all the way to McDonald's. At least their stuff looked like it hadn't been frozen for months.

The first person he saw in the lineup (looking terribly out of place with a trayful of garden salads) was his father. Jackson did a U-turn and bolted out the door.

He stumbled around, confused, not knowing to where he should look for relief. He ran mentally through a checklist of his favorite foods. Maybe pizza would do the trick.

He made it finally to a place called Masterpizza, his mind and stomach a mess. He didn't recognize the name, but he went inside anyway, submitting to a need greater than the comfort of a known brand name.

As soon as he walked through the door the place erupted into a wild spectacle of flashing lights and cheering customers.

"You won! You won!"

"I what?"

An older woman, short and stocky, burst through the kitchen door. "Good heavens!" she cried. "Jackson!"

"Mrs. Landsberg?" He hardly recognized the missing librarian without a book in her hand.

"You won, Jackson, you're the 028 customer! You won!"

"Huh?"

"028 — it's my all-time favorite Dewey Decimal number, the one for Reading. And you're it. You won the grand-opening prize!"

That did little to lessen his confusion. It was only when Mrs. Landsberg told him she had given up her work at the library to open a pizza house that he began to get a reasonable grip on it all. He glanced around the room as she explained how she had decided to create the look of a library, with shelves along the walls stocked tightly with books, and framed pictures of Canadian authors above the cash register. The placemats had reproductions of the opening pages of famous novels.

"Masterpizza," she said, with a little Italian accent. "Get it?"

After a while he got it and laughed along with her.

"*It's too mucha for words*. That's our motto."

After a while he got that too and laughed again.

"It's the thinking person's pizza house, Jackson. It's not part of any franchise. I thought it up myself, with a little help from my husband," she said, turning to Mr. Landsberg, who had just emerged from the kitchen, his hands covered in flour.

"It's terrific, it really is," Jackson said, the thrill of it all beginning to show in his voice.

"We can't just stand here," Mr. Landsberg said excitedly. "Give him the prize. It's real gold, Jackson."

Jackson could hardly believe his eyes as they brought it to him, in a miniature cardboard pizza box, the inside lined with velvet. Resting on the velvet was a gold medal — in the shape of a pizza, right down to the lip of crust and delicately embossed mushrooms and pepperoni.

"And anchovies," Mrs. Landsberg said, beaming. "See, right there."

Jackson picked up the medal and held it between his thumb and forefinger. He hardly knew what to say.

"It's a real work of art," he said finally.

"It cost quite a bit, but we really did want to make the

prize special. And it couldn't have gone to a nicer guy."

They hugged each other.

"Bring on the pizza," Mr. Landsberg said, breaking it up. "The poor guy looks like he's starved. What'll you have, Jackson? It's on us."

Jackson checked the menu.

"The Dickens Special sounds good."

"Very filling, but a great choice."

He sat down among the other customers, many of whom had gone back to their pizzas and books. What a terrific concept, he was thinking. Library science will never be the same.

A half hour later, his great gastronomic expectations satisfied, he headed home and slithered into the house. He was dying to tell his mother, but he knew he couldn't mention eating out for fear she would call him a traitor to the cause.

He walked into the living room as if he had just come down from upstairs. Katherine was sitting there in her dressing gown with a cup of herbal tea, rereading one of her Margaret Atwood novels. Jackson sat down quietly.

"Kath, sorry I got mad," he said.

She looked at him, relieved, too, to be making amends. She smiled softly. "I understand. I know you have a lot on your mind."

"Any sign it might be working?"

"It's still too early."

He didn't have the stomach to tell her where he had been or whom he had seen at McDonald's.

"What's he trying to prove, Jackson?"

"I don't know. But I'm sure we'll get to him sooner or later."

"I hope you're right. I can't take much more."

"Neither can I."

He had to give his mother more than just words. He stared forthrightly at the titles of his father's cherished leather-bound, gold-edged collection. Dare he choose one and forcefully extract it? Get to his father where it really hurt? How glaring a hole could he create? Without any thought of his actions being anything other than an outstanding show of solidarity for his mother, his eyes fell on *The Odyssey* by Homer. Ancient Greece! He could be defiant and practical at the same time. Perfect!

He pulled the book from its comfortable little row. He turned to his mother, the book under his arm, his hands in his pockets. He gave her a smile that was worth a thousand apologies. He said nothing more, just strolled to the foot of the stairs, then climbed them slowly, precisely, as if he were being filled with the power of the written word. It drew him higher and higher, until finally he made it to his bedroom.

There he lay on his back across the bed, his head propped up with a couple of pillows. He rubbed his fingers shamelessly against the leather, then flipped the book into the air, catching it with his other hand.

He stretched the book open at random, taking particular pleasure in gliding the fingers of one hand along the golden edges of the paper. Then, resting the book against his legs, he took the pizza medal from its box and rubbed it with the fingers of his other hand to compare the feel of the two. His eyes fixed for a second on the poster of Gauguin's golden girls.

He turned to the words in the book. Suddenly he had the strangest feeling, as if a circle of warmth were hovering just over his head. He wanted to search out the reason for it, but found he could not take his eyes off the book. It was the part where Odysseus and his men are trapped in the cave with Cyclops, the one-eyed monster.

He felt his eyelids turn heavy. The warm glow was descending down the rest of his body and out into the farthest reaches of his limbs. When it reached his fingertips there was a wonderful sensation through all his body, not unlike some he had known before, but made all the better because he didn't feel the least bit guilty about it.

"Holy shiiit!" he moaned.

He was left with a terrific afterglow and a longing to sleep.

THREE

A smell, worse than a locker room after the sweatiest of basketball games, drifted into his nostrils. He could feel the pizza medal still between his fingers. He forced it down the back pocket of his jeans. He opened his eyes.

"Hoooly shit!" he groaned.

Jackson found himself crouched down on his knees, pinned against the rock wall of a huge cave. Squashed against him were the bodies of three foul-smelling brutes of men, crouching too, and wolfing in air like they were scared out of their minds of something. But no way could they be any more terrified than he was of them — shoulder muscles broader than their heads and weird clothes and looking as though they were hiding weapons! Maybe they were professional wrestlers. But God, he was thinking, his personal life couldn't be that bad that he'd have a dream like this!

Suddenly, one of the brutes jabbed an elbow into his gut, and Jackson quickly realized it was no dream.

And if he was terrified then, it was nothing to what he felt when through the opening of the cave he saw a brute ten times the size and ugliness of any one of the others. Not just ugliness, but nothing between his mountainous nose and the wall of his forehead except ONE enormous eyeball.

Someone had got to be kidding! Jackson sucked down the deepest breath he had ever taken and shut his eyes and wished with every ounce of life in him that it was only a good Steven Spielberg movie.

He scraped his head against the rock wall and flicked open his eyes. Nothing had changed. Except now he saw the one-eyed ogre driving a bunch of oversized sheep and goats into the cave. And once inside, the brute picked up a huge rock — which Jackson hoped could be no more than a realistic chunk of Styrofoam — and tossed it down to block the entrance. Jackson's teeth rattled! No special effects could be that good. This was no movie!

Just what was going on? Had he, by some force beyond all the known laws of the universe, been yanked out of his own century, transported back to ancient Greece, and dumped in the midst of the book he had been reading? He had heard of getting caught up in a good story, but wasn't this getting a bit too carried away?

He started to laugh it off as a ridiculous warp of a fertile imagination. But the way the sheep and goats were blaring their lungs out, it was proving difficult to do. And there was no way he could ignore what was definitely the slosh of liquid. The poor beasts — he had to pity them if they were being milked by hands as calloused and clumsy as those.

Imagine what they could do to a human's neck! His eyes bulged at the thought. He sunk his head as far down as he could get it. If it all was for real, then it was better to die of body odor, crushed between muscle and rock than to come eye-to-eye with that monstrous torturer.

After a while the animal noises changed to what seemed more normal sounds to be coming from sheep and goats. It gave Jackson a chance to calm himself. He bravely squirmed into a new position and peered out through the legs of whoever was piled against him.

The monster let loose an ungodly roar. The blasting pain in

Jackson's ears was exactly what he needed to finally admit that this really was one gigantic screw-up that wasn't going to go away.

He did find some consolation in the fact that there were other people about, in another part of the cave. He could hear their voices, though what they were saying was all Greek to him. So maybe there were a lot more humans for the Cyclops to get through before it reached him. Jackson buried his head in his hands and prayed that he would be spared whatever it was that was going through the monster's mind.

He heard the word *Zeus* among all the gibberish echoing through the cave. Oh no, maybe he had been praying to the wrong god? It wasn't fair. How was he supposed to know what to do? He tried desperately to remember what he had learned of ancient history. All he could think of was Apollo and space ships and astronauts. He did know a lot about the Olympic Games. Maybe if he built a prayer around that then Zeus would be more likely to listen.

Before he had time to decide just how he was going to word it, the Cyclops jumped up from beside the fire and lunged both his massive paws at the men crowded against Jackson. They drew back every last inch they could. On the retreat, one of them caught Jackson with a knee square in the side of the mouth.

There wasn't room for Jackson to breathe, let alone get a hand to his sore jaw. But then, just as he thought he would pass out, he got more breathing space than he ever wanted. The feet and legs smothering him, and the bodies to which they were attached, were all of a sudden no longer there, and he had a clear, unobstructed view of just where they ended up. The ogre had plucked them away and now they were squirming like crazy, one in each of his hands. He raised them high over his head and laughed sickeningly, then flung them to the ground.

Jackson snapped his eyes shut. Just the thud of their bodies against rock was bad enough. He covered his ears and begged forgiveness to whomever was listening for all the pleasure he had ever derived from reading the books of Stephen King. He vowed that if he could be spared he would never buy another one again, no matter how out of it it would make him feel.

When he did finally open his eyes, after swearing off every bad habit he had (and some that he wasn't so sure about but wasn't willing to take any chances with), he saw no maimed bodies, only the leg that had smacked him in the face a few minutes before. He saw it disappear into the Cyclopean gob as the beast slurped it up like a strand of spaghetti, then wiped away the red stuff dripping from his lips. It gave Jackson a new understanding of the word *gross*.

Was he to go the same way? Was he to have no more purpose than to be food for some brute bigger and stronger than himself? He suddenly had sympathy for all the meat he had ever eaten. He shut his eyes tightly again. Please, O Supreme Being, he implored, spare me and I will become an animal rights activist.

The others shushed him into silence. He hadn't realized he was praying out loud. He looked about the cave. The Cyclops was lying among the sheep, resting after his inhumanness. Jackson's prayers had been answered. Either that or the guy was letting his stomach settle before dessert.

Eventually the fire died away, and in time Jackson could hear only the wretched rumble of the ogre's guts and then the fitful snores of his heavy sleep. The men from the different parts of the cave gathered around him and the others who were left uneaten. They whispered in earnest. Jackson mumbled about in the dark, trying desperately to be one of the crowd. If it was escape they were planning, he had to be part of it.

There was one who talked like he was the leader. Jackson recognized the uncontrollable heroism in his voice. Odysseus, they called him. If there was anyone who would save him, he was the guy. Zeus, dear Zeus, Jackson muttered to himself, let it be so.

For a time Jackson lost hope that Odysseus could indeed get him out of this mess. The men had scattered back to the corners of the cave, waiting for daylight. Jackson thought it a rather gutless thing to do, although he was in no position to argue. He could do nothing but follow and crouch away in dread, as far from the snoring of the Cyclops as he could get.

Dawn came, and before the monster left for the hills with the sheep and goats, he snatched up two more unfortunate souls and gobbled them down for his breakfast. The swipe of his hand had again come dangerously close to Jackson. Another meal and he would be done for, Jackson thought. Unless that Odysseus could get his act together, come nightfall he would be history, and ancient history at that.

He should not have lost faith in the man. For, as soon as the hulk had left the cave and rolled the rock back across the entrance, Odysseus was calling to the men excitedly with what could only be plans to get them out of the slaughter pen.

Jackson decided it was best to stay put and hope the dim light was not enough to reveal what he was wearing. How could he ever look like one of the crowd dressed in jeans and a sweatshirt that said "The Pepsi Generation"? Among all those leather sandals strapped up their legs, and chest protectors and funny short skirts, he would never pass for the real thing. They had beards and lots of hair all over their bodies; he had only the stuff he was trying to grow on his top lip. Besides, most of them had muscles big enough to make Sylvester Stallone look puny. And they could even make their grunts sound intelligent.

No, he wasn't about to chance it. He'd stay where he was and make his move when the right time came. He had no trouble understanding their scheme, however. Anyone would have been able to see by the way they were grunting what they had in mind. Odysseus had cut off a section of a dry log to about the length of a man, and now the others were cutting away the bark and sharpening the end to a fine point. A massive spear to drive into a massive heart! A courageous plan, thought Jackson, if they did succeed in killing the monster while he slept, how would they ever move that cursed rock? Bet they hadn't thought of that, he grieved. No worse to die as food than die of starvation.

By the time the evening came and the Cyclops returned to the cave with his flock, Jackson had resigned himself to death. He had made his peace with the world, such as it had come to be. A bizarre end it would be to a fellow named Jackson. He savored every last lungful of oxygen. As the monster milked his tormented animals, Jackson drifted into a stupor. He dreamed he was still in New York City.

The Cyclops let free a thunderous belch, and, snapping back to the unreal world, Jackson knew he wasn't the meal the ogre was belching about. He had not been supper. Zeus was clearly working in mysterious ways.

He heard the voice of Odysseus, and in the firelight Jackson could see that he was cautiously putting within the Cyclops's reach a bowl filled with a dark liquid. The monster grabbed it and drank it down with great gusto, then belched again. Jackson instantly realized that it was wine. It smelled like the stuff they served in the economy section of airplanes.

After two refills of the bowl, the wine was too much for even a giant's nervous system and he fell polluted back to the floor of the cave and into a noisy sleep. He snorted and belched some more and threw up bits of leather and other fleshy stuff that Jackson wished he hadn't seen.

Meanwhile, as quickly as possible Odysseus and four of his men retrieved the sharpened stick from where they had hidden it in a pile of dung. They stuck its point into the embers of the fire and left it there until it too glowed red with the heat.

Then, with the courage and fury of a dozen stallions, they drove the searing, shitty end of the stick at the Cyclops, into his eye! The eye! Quick thinking, Odysseus! Jackson silently cheered.

They turned it round and round, driving it deeper and deeper into the eyeball. The thunderous bellow that erupted from the Cyclops was like nothing Jackson had ever heard. The most popular heavy metal band could not have produced such a cry of agony. It sent the torturers fleeing to all parts of the cave. Pulling loose the bloody stake, the Cyclops flung it to the wall. A trail of blood whipped across Jackson's face. The monster screamed still louder. Jackson wiped his face and covered his ears and longed for the quiet of home, with nothing more amplified than Roger Whittaker or Barry Manilow to break the silence.

Feeling about until he found the rock that blocked the entrance to the cave, the monster cast it spitefully to one side. The light of a full moon spread into the cave. He stretched his murderous forelimbs to where the rock had been, to stop anyone who dared think it possible to escape. Jackson cursed him in his own inaudible way.

Even in this revengeful scheme of the Cyclops, Odysseus was not to be outsmarted. While the monster whined like a pitbull terrier with a cut paw, Odysseus was getting his men to tie rams together in groups of three. A confusing activity at the best of times, but Jackson was sure it had a brilliant purpose.

And indeed it had! For against the underbelly of the middle of each three, he then tied a man. Soon every one of them, except Odysseus and himself, was ram shackled and ready. For what, Jackson wasn't quite sure, but he had to be part of it. It was his only hope.

So, mustering all the courage that had been building inside him, he stepped out in full view of Odysseus.

Odysseus drew back as if he were seeing an extra-terrestrial being. Jackson thought it a bit of an overreaction, especially after being caged up with a Cyclops for two days. Odysseus sized him up. Jackson tried his best to look as though he belonged. He threw out his chest even farther and gave a Rambo-like look of disgust toward the Cyclops. Odysseus looked even more confused. He gestured to Jackson with his right hand. What it meant, Jackson had no idea.

"Alpha?" Jackson said in his best and only Greek.

The Cyclops roared at the sound of a human voice. Jackson raced to an empty ram near Odysseus and threw his arms around its neck and curled his body against its underbelly. He looked sheepishly into Odysseus's eyes, praying that he show him pity. The monster roared again. Odysseus, perhaps not willing to take a chance on angering some god, quickly tied Jackson to the ram and then tied another ram to each side. At last Jackson felt like one of the crowd.

It was a long, though not entirely uncomfortable, wait. Jackson was cosily warm. At least one side of him was. And the ram seemed happy enough, once Jackson learned not to move his feet.

When the sun rose the rams began to stir about, anxious to be back to their pastureland. It suddenly dawned on Jackson just what the great Odysseus had in mind. This wasn't just his way of hiding the men from the revengeful fury of the beast. Praise Zeus!

As the rams jostled out through the opening, the muttering Cyclops pawed them over, but without discovering what human hearts beat down below. Soon they were out into the broad blue daylight. Free at last! Free at last! They had certainly pulled the wool over his eye, Jackson chuckled to himself.

Jackson squirmed about, eager to get really free. The sheep to which he was so attached began to lick Jackson's face in a deliberate show of affection, then turned to bleating impatiently, as if to suggest that the other two rams should get lost. Jackson started to sweat profusely as his mind wandered in unpleasant directions. Eventually, Odysseus came to his rescue. He freed the rams from each other, and then, after some difficulty in getting the middle one to calm himself, he cut away Jackson's hands and feet.

Jackson dropped to the ground and scurried out from under the beast. The animal wandered away, dejected and thoroughly confused by human nature. Jackson was immensely relieved. He reached out for Odysseus's hand to thank him, but the hero quickly drew away. He gathered together his men, every one of whom stared at Jackson wide-eyed and speechless.

Was there no way for Jackson to show that he was part of

their world, that he was to be trusted? He dared not make any signs with his hands for fear they would be misinterpreted. He searched his pockets for a peace offering. A package of breath mints? There were only three pieces left, not enough for all of them. And what if they didn't like the flavor of retsyn — might they think he was trying to poison them?

The Cyclops was growing restless inside the cave. Odysseus and his men would not be waiting much longer. The back pocket of Jackson's jeans offered up the gold pizza medal. He held it in the palm of his outstretched hand and walked toward them. The embossed mushrooms, pepperoni and anchovies gleamed in the sunlight. The Greeks' distrust of Jackson slowly subsided, and when he stood before them and held the coin up for Odysseus to take, there was an exchange of smiles and an understanding that did not need words. Jackson, the late-twentieth-century adolescent, paying homage to the ancient, but truly awesome, hero, Odysseus. He couldn't help but think what a terrific video it would have made.

Odysseus took from a pouch at his side a piece of what had to be gold too, smiled and held it out to Jackson. Jackson's fingertips went to the roughly shaped piece, and at the same time he held out the pizza medal with the fingertips of his other hand to place it in the outstretched palm of Odysseus.

He felt his legs suddenly turn weak. They would not hold him upright. Odysseus's face turned to nothing but an after-image behind eyes that Jackson could not keep open. His body sagged to the ground, and he felt himself drifting away.

Away, so far away. Only the distant roar of the Cyclops could he hear. Finally that, too, was gone. Relief mixed with a certain regret. He had so wanted Odysseus to be a friend, not just someone who saved his life.

Ultimately, the relief and the regret, these, too, were gone. He sensed nothing for a length of time to which even a Rolex could not do justice.

FOUR

He blinked a few more times and looked at his watch. He saw that it had moved only three or four minutes — just the time it took to read a few pages.

He snapped the book shut. Staring about the room, he saw Gauguin's girls looking at him from the wall, and he felt the old stir of interest. He touched himself all over, some places repeatedly, just to make sure he was all there. He really was back from wherever in the name of whatever god he had been.

He sat up, then quickly stood up. He relaxed his sweaty fist and looked at what he had been holding so incredibly tightly. It was the pizza medal. He kept looking at it, not sure what to think, not sure if it wouldn't suddenly do something on its own, like turn extraordinarily bright and cast a magical aura about the room. It did nothing of the sort.

Nevertheless, he found a special spot in the far reaches of his closet where no one would discover it — the same spot where he kept a trio of condoms. They had been there for so long he'd been thinking he might have to replace them, since he wasn't sure they could still do the job. Not that he had any chance of finding out very soon. But that was another matter, one he was surprised he could even think about after what he had gone through. It went to show just how normal he really was again.

But just what, in fact, *had* he gone through? A daydream of unusually vivid proportions? A hallucinogenic stupor?

No, he was thinking, it was a hell of a lot more than that. It was an absolutely all-out, full-scale out-of-the-body experience. People who read the *National Enquirer* had told him about things like this happening. He was ashamed now he had ever laughed at them. Or laughed at his mother for reading Shirley MacLaine, for that matter.

He left his room, his head awhirl with headlines that could sell a million newspapers. By the time he got to the living room and saw his mother still sitting there, he was already planning that first date with whomever Hollywood would hire to play his girlfriend in the movie.

Katherine looked up. "That was quick. Couldn't bring yourself to actually read it, could you? Jackson, I mean business. Things have got to change around here."

He wasn't listening to a word she was saying. He stared lovingly at her and, without any control over himself at all, he wrapped his arms around her and held her more tightly than he had done in years. "Kath, it's so good to see you."

She was pleasantly surprised, of course. Even more so when he didn't say a word about borrowing the car. He hugged her so long that she finally had to force them apart. "Jackson, is something the matter? Whatever it is, it can't be that bad."

"Kath, it was."

"What was?"

"It was horrible."

He proceeded to tell her the whole story.

She listened. She kept herself completely under control until the part about being tied up under the ram, and then she broke into wild, almost hysterical, laughter.

He got mad with her, but it did no good. She couldn't stop herself.

"Jackson," she finally managed to get out between the last spurts of laughter, "that's wild. For heaven's sake, get it down on paper. You could sell that to the *National Enquirer* and make a bloody fortune!"

He left the room in disgust.

For several hours afterwards all that he had on his mind was what he could do to make someone believe him. Maybe he had imagined it? But he was positive he hadn't. He'd bet his turbulent teenage life on it.

But he also knew that there was no one who would take him seriously. And to think that he'd have to go through life a prisoner to such a secret. As a last resort, he could write Ann Landers, he supposed. Or see a psychiatrist. There had to be psychiatrists who would believe him. He might have to pay dearly for it, but he was sure they were out there somewhere.

For now, he'd have to learn to live with it all, just like he did with the longing to be in New York. Life was cruel, and getting crueller by the hour.

When he heard his father come home he didn't even bother leaving his bedroom to try to tell him. It would be impossible to convince his father that he was being dead serious for once. It could only further complicate their relationship.

He would be on shaky ground with him as it was, what with the book in his room. Most likely Katherine had told his father where it was; he would have noticed it missing from the shelf as soon as he stepped into the living room. And Jackson knew, too, it would have to stay there or his mother would think him gutless.

On her way to the spare bedroom, where she had moved after the flare-up in the kitchen, she stopped in to see him.

"By the time I was your age I had already taken part in three sit-ins, almost got arrested, and joined the New Democratic Party," she said, in a tone meant to be reassuring.

"So?"

"So, don't cop out when the going gets tough."

"Cop out?"

"Wimp out. For heaven's sake, don't wimp out."

If there was anything he wasn't going to be called by his own mother, it was a wimp.

"Katherine," he said, "I do have other problems to deal with, you know. This is not the only thing that happens to be on my mind. I've got this oral report to give tomorrow morning. I've got two exams on Monday to study for. And a term paper due in next week which I haven't even started yet. Plus I've been playing lousy basketball lately and I might just get dropped from the team. Plus I got this body that I can't keep under control. And now I have a mother who calls me a wimp."

She didn't say anything. The tilt of her head said it all.

He continued while the going was good. "When was the last time you had to worry about not having a date for Saturday night? When was the last time you woke up with zits rearing their ugly heads on the side of your nose?"

"Sorry," she said. There was a meaningful pause. "But I'm pretty desperate."

"So am I. But let's face it, what did your militancy get you before? The world is not exactly overflowing with peace and love and harmony. The Beatles' music is selling beer and sneakers. Charlie Brown is selling insurance. Jane Fonda is selling herself."

He left his mother stammering for a defense and took off downstairs. He flicked on the TV, only to find Bill Cosby staring back at him. Just how many bloody sweaters did that man own!

He snapped it off and sought refuge in the refrigerator. What he found there was a sad display of the extremes to which his mother was willing to go to get her point across to his father. Gone was anything that resembled the fresh and healthy items that normally filled the shelves, replaced by a sickly collection of products made by the company his father worked for. Jackson could never have imagined such a heartless, deliberate show of bad taste. The shelves were a mass of the microwavable. He picked up a package of something called Deli-Style Miniburgers. He recalled his father's enthusiasm for the ad: "Now you've got it all, even the pickle."

He slammed the refrigerator door and went to sleep hungry.

And woke up hungry, having fallen asleep across the bed while trying to make notes for his report on ancient Greece. His clock radio read 7:40. He was due to give his class presentation in one hour and twenty minutes.

Regardless of the consequences, though, he just had to have something in his gut. He showed up in the kitchen and resigned himself to some pre-fab thing in a pouch that supposedly turned to food in thirty seconds.

As he bit into it, his mother cringed with satisfaction at his demonstration of loyalty to her.

"Jackson, what happened to you?" she said, noticing for the first time the state of his clothing.

"Slept in my clothes. That's all."

"That wouldn't happen if you wore synthetics," his father said. "Cotton is hell for wrinkles."

How insensitive! How dated! Jackson felt like telling him just how close he had come to losing his darling son the night before. How all he might have been left with was the imprint of his son's body on a permapress bedspread.

"Ever think I might go somewhere and not want to come back?" Jackson said, restraining himself with great difficulty.

"Like where — the refrigerator?" his father replied.

When nobody else even smiled, his father said, "Get serious."

"It just might happen. Then you would be sorry."

"Sorry for what, Jackson love?" his mother asked, trying to help him make his point.

"Sorry for ever having me."

He could be cruel when he got desperate.

Unfortunately, his father didn't see it as desperation. He saw it as Jackson's way of trying to get around him, to get him to give in to the trip back to New York.

"You don't mean that," his father said, looking him straight in the eye and putting his hand on Jackson's shoulder. "I know you don't. If you did, I'd be heartbroken."

Heartbroken? And the damned thing was he meant it. So his father did love him. And he loved Katherine, too. The problem was he was so out of touch with reality that he was constantly misinterpreting the emotional cues being directed toward him.

Or so his mother said afterwards. She had read a lot of self-help books and even subscribed to *Psychology Today* for a year.

Katherine and Jackson were edging toward the limits of their endurance. She even said, after his father left for work, that she could see the possibility of a severing of familial ties, a realignment of the family structure.

"God, Katherine, can't you come right out and say it."

"Okay, okay! Two weeks and that's it. If he doesn't come around by then, I'm going to up and leave him, and take you with me."

Jackson felt sick. He thought his family was made of tougher stuff. They shouldn't have to take the easy way out, no matter what the other half of the population was doing. He always wanted to be different. He didn't want to be adding to the percentage of broken homes. Families living together and trying to sort out their problems because they loved each other had always appealed to him. It made him think that if enough people did it, politicians might try it too, and then they could take what they learned to global conferences and the world would become like a family.

Far-fetched, he knew. Probably not good for the economy. Probably drive inflation and interest rates right through the ozone layer. And everybody knew nobody was going to be happy unless they had lots of money.

He was getting carried away. He had to focus his attention on coming up with a solution for his own family.

But even that had to take second place for the moment. The class presentation was where his mind had to be. He had time only to scrawl a few more words on an index card before showering and dressing for school. His appearance would be just as important as what he would say. He had watched enough TV news to know that.

When he entered the classroom he immediately spotted Sara. She looked so fresh and full of fun that he felt weak with excitement at the prospect of their being together. She glanced at him, then turned back to what she was doing. That brief but deceptively vague look, the way her eyes had swept across his — it said it all. He could tell she wanted him more than she was ever willing to let him know.

He was going to meet all her expectations, surpass them as a matter of fact. He had ten minutes in which to do it.

And indeed, it flowed out so smoothly, so confidently, that the time just flew by. Of course, what he offered was a particularly realistic perspective of Odysseus's encounter with the Cyclops. He went on and on in the most enlightening detail about how it must have felt to be trapped inside a cave with such a loathsome monster. In fact, the teacher had to remind him twice to wrap it up because he had gone overtime trying to squeeze in all he could about the sheer and absolute courage of those in the cave who faced the brute. He did manage to leave the class with a picture of exactly how tough *he* would have been. He smiled gently at Sara and walked fearlessly back to his seat.

He could see she was impressed beyond words. The teacher said that he had done an intriguing job in making the story come alive, that he made them all appreciate the tremendous power of myth. The teacher's voice definitely had the ring of an A+.

When the bell went for the end of class, Jackson knew it was the moment for him to make his big move. He timed his departure to coincide precisely with Sara's.

He gave her a carefree but confident "Hi." It had an intellectual edge to it.

"Hi," she said back to him, with a hint of a smile that he could just tell was dying to spread lovingly across her face.

His next line, he knew, was all-important. It came to him in a flash of inspiration. "Want to go somewhere sometime and share a bottle of wine and talk?" It was the artist in him coming through.

She didn't answer. He looked ahead of him and saw why. There was Adam.

"Hi," Adam said to Sara.

Was that all the guy could come up with? Jackson thought. Or was putting more than one word together in the right order too much for his brain to handle?

"Want to get together for lunch? After school I have a chess club meeting and then I should work out for a while in the weight room. The all-star game is tomorrow."

Man, how sickening! Jackson just knew that underneath that polite exterior there lurked someone with the vainness of a model for designer underwear. How could a couple be so incompatible and not realize it? It made Jackson want to strip away the act that excuse for a boyfriend was putting on and show him up for the fake that he was. The only reason he didn't do it right there and then was because he didn't want to embarrass Sara.

He tried to ignore Adam standing there, except, of course, when the guy said, "Hi, how's it goin', man? I heard someone say you gave a great presentation."

He knew he would have to say something, for the sake of Sara's feelings. "It went okay."

"C'mon, man, you're just being modest."

Unlike some people, Jackson was tempted to fire back at him.

"He was great," Sara said.

Suddenly it was as if the sky opened up and an angel had passed judgment on his whole being. She had said "great"! She had thrown open the door of opportunity and invited him in.

"You really were," she said.

He was cast into a sea of ecstasy, left to drown in it as Sara and Adam walked away.

He floated through the corridors to his next class. It was

math. A lost cause. He couldn't control his equations. They kept wandering off into new and unverifiable directions. By the end of class he was feverish with desire to give it all up and go off to lunch.

The cafeteria was offering up what it delighted in calling Saucy Meatloaf. Jackson was sure it was the administration's way of getting back at unruly students. It was a slight step up from what he had to suffer through at home, and fortunately he had something to take his mind off the way the meatloaf tended to ooze uncontrollably about the plate.

He sat himself at a table not far from Adam and Sara to reinforce in her mind the fact that he was thinking about her. He knew better than to make direct eye contact with them. That would only put unnecessary thoughts in Adam's head. Instead, he sat with his back to them, forcing himself to eat as quietly as he could, hoping to catch the thought-provoking sound of her voice.

He loved the rhythm of her words near him, even though after a few minutes they came laced with anger and frustration. She was mad about something. From what he could hear it seemed that a book that was to be studied in her English class had been withdrawn because someone had complained about its contents.

"I've seen it before," she said. "Censorship, that's what it is."

It was a foul, unpleasant word that reeked of unfairness. Coming from such wonderful lips, it seemed to him even worse. He hated the thought that she was so in need of comfort and he could do nothing about it right at that moment.

"The parent is calling it racist and sexist," Sara said. "She's saying it's full of negative images of blacks and women."

"It does use 'nigger' a lot, and I couldn't find any strong female characters," Adam said.

"It's a reflection of American society at the time it was written," Sara countered.

Of course it is! Jackson thought it ridiculously dumb of Adam not to see that. He loved the tone of impatience in Sara's voice. He only wished he knew what book it was she was talking about.

Her intelligence was so overpowering in comparison to Adam's that Jackson wondered how in the name of heaven she could stand going out with the guy. Jackson sat in anxious anticipation of what kind of idiot remark the guy was going to come up with next.

"Sara, there's no need to get so worked up about it."

Idiot! She's worked up about it because she has to be worked up about it. She's a compassionate young woman who rages against injustice. Of course she's worked up about it. What intelligent person wouldn't be?

"I can't help it," she said. "It just infuriates me."

Me too, Jackson thought. It makes my blood boil.

Sara and Adam finished what they were eating and got up from their seats. They walked toward the exit. "Imagine," she said, "high school students not being allowed to study *Huck Finn*. It makes my blood boil."

He and Sara were meant for each other, he knew it.

But *Huck Finn*. She had to be kidding. Yet that's what she had said. It was a classic. It was on his father's bookshelf. One of "the greatest literary works of all time." He couldn't believe it. He had additional trouble getting down the last of his dessert.

He rushed home after school and pulled the book down from the living-room shelf. He looked through it gingerly, being careful to avoid any movement of his fingers along the golden edges of the paper. He didn't want to take any chances on finding himself up the Mississippi without a paddle.

It didn't take Jackson long to see that Sara had every reason to be mad. (He had never actually read the book. He had heard a lot about it and he had seen the movie on television, and read the comic when he was younger, but he had never really gotten around to the actual words.) When he did start reading it, right there in the living room in his father's chair, he couldn't put it down. He could hardly believe that a classic could be so good.

There was a lot of the "n" word, but no more than he knew he would have heard if he'd been living when Twain wrote the book. And Aunt Sally and the Widow Douglas and Miss Watson weren't exactly free spirits, but they sure showed how much things had changed since then.

His mother showed up as if to prove the point. "What's for dinner?" she called from inside the front door.

It was her attempt at humor, of course. She knew there was nothing, other than whatever preserved excuse-for-food was in the refrigerator. What chemical concoction was there to wreak havoc with his taste buds tonight, he wondered.

"You tell me," he called back to her.

She was delighted to find Jackson reclining so comfortably in his father's chair and so deeply absorbed in one of his books.

"Food for thought?" she said.

"Please, Katherine. There's nothing I hate worse than a joke at my stomach's expense."

"Tell you what," she said cheerfully, "tonight we'll have Breast of Chicken Terre-Neuvien."

He couldn't believe his ears. His mouth began to water immediately. "What happened? Did someone buy one of those moose paintings or what?"

"Your father's secretary called to say that he wouldn't be home till late." She held up a grocery bag. "We've got four hours before he gets here."

"Great!"

It was like old times. Real food cooking in a real oven, giving off unsimulated smells. It made life livable again.

He ate and ate and ate. He felt just like his old teenage self.

It was great to be on good terms with his mother again. They even shared a bottle of the imported beer she had been saving for the day his father gave in and started cooking.

"Does this mean you're giving up on him?" he asked,

expecting the worst.

"No way. This is just to give me strength to go on," she said, drinking straight out of the bottle and laughing.

As much as she was enjoying the beer, he knew there was no cause for alarm. Alcohol was not something she would resort to, no matter how much better the life in the beer commercials on TV.

He talked to his mother about the book and the complaints that were being leveled against it. She, too, found it hard to think that Mark Twain would set out to poison anybody's mind.

"I read that book when I was your age," she said. "Look at me. I don't have a prejudiced bone in my body."

He knew she didn't like boxing, or seeing Bill Cosby in so many ads, but then again he knew love of money wasn't particularly a black trait.

"And as for the picture of women it presents, from what I remember most of the men weren't exactly role models, unless you consider lying and cheating and drunkenness to be male virtues."

Strong words. It was her Sixties nature coming through again, the years of standing up for her own and other people's rights. It made Jackson proud of her. And envious. He wished he could be growing up at a time when society had more on its mind than the value of the Japanese yen and the intricacies of Madonna's love life.

Suddenly it struck him. There *was* something he could stand up for! Freedom to read. He could talk to Sara and tell her how concerned he was about the infringement of rights that was taking place. Tell her that what they had to do was organize a protest — together. That together they would beat this thing, squelch it before it threatened the very foundations of their way of life. They would restore the democratic right of every individual to have free and open access to books for whatever purpose they desired. He would do all that, and he would win the girl.

Sara would be his. No Adam could ever survive such a display of self-sacrifice for the good of the world.

He drank some more of the imported beer and basked in the thoughts of his plan.

"You look awfully pleased with yourself," his mother commented.

"Just thinking about something."

"Someone, you mean."

"How can you tell?" he said.

"I was in love once, too, you know."

"And you will be again."

"Do you really think so?"

"You know what they always say — the tougher the fight, the sweeter the prize."

She smiled as though his words were vaguely familiar. "Let's hope so," she said.

As they cleared away the dishes and returned the kitchen to its normal sterile self, there was a sudden, brief moment when Jackson felt intensely sad. It pained him to think that his family had come to this — using food as a weapon, cooking behind one another's backs, then destroying the evidence. It smelled of ethical decay, poisonous behavior that had no place in the world of the family.

His father came into the house just as the last dish was being put away. Jackson felt like a weight-lifter at the Olympics.

"Anything left?" his father asked as he walked into the kitchen.

"Food, you mean?" his mother said icily.

There was a long, unpleasant silence. His father continued on to the refrigerator, as his mother went past Jackson and into the living room.

Jackson turned to follow her, but then stopped and looked back at his father.

"Dad, you won't find much in there."

"Except my life's work." He stared at Jackson. He was troubled.

Jackson stared back at him with the hope that it would cause him to undertake some new and affirmative action. His father opened the refrigerator and took out a package, a three-minute stir-fry with rice.

Jackson turned away again, sorry he had even tried. He retrieved the copy of *Huckleberry Finn* and escaped up the stairs to his room.

FIVE

He kept his bedroom door locked for hours. But he knew there was no way to really shut it all out. The stench of irreconcilable differences was everywhere in the house. On top of all his other problems — the unrequited love, the mound of schoolwork still undone, the ever-present threat of acne — there was his family with less than two weeks before self-destruction. He felt as though he was trapped in a young adult novel.

But he did have an escape. He had this way into another world that no one knew about, his little pressure-release valve that could send him off into adventures that made his own problems look like the stuff of foreign-language films.

Dare he try it again? Would it work a second time? Dare he enter with abandon a world from which there might be no escape? He was depressed about his problems, but did he need to resort to literal suicide?

The answer was a resounding "no."

Not unless there was a guarantee he would return and be able to claim Sara as his prize. The tangible results of his previous little odyssey had not quite been what he imagined. It hadn't exactly driven a wedge between her and Adam.

No, he would have to rely on more conventional methods to make her see the light. He would stick with his original plan. He would phone her up and spill out all his heartfelt concerns about the vicious threat to their freedom to read, and assure her he would be responsive to any and all of her suggestions about what, between them, they could do.

He was not the least bit hesitant in phoning. He had none of the nervousness that normally plagues adolescent young men when they call adolescent young women for the first time. He couldn't see that there was anything to get nervous about. He was sure he couldn't possibly make a fool of himself.

Unfortunately, the line was busy. He tried again, then several times more, each time with a little more frustration.

At first he wouldn't let it cross his mind that Adam talking to her might be the reason he couldn't get through. It wasn't worthy of a thought. But as time went on and his fingers started getting tired pressing the same buttons, he was forced to let it occur to him that this was a remote possibility.

By the tenth time dialing, he was ready to throttle the guy. What right did he think he had hogging the line? What if there was some emergency? Someone's life could be at stake, and here was this lymph node tying up the phone line like he owned the damned thing. Inconsiderate was too good a word for it.

Suddenly the rings went through. Jackson panicked. What was he going to say? His mind was a blank. It was just like that jerk Adam to hang up so unexpectedly. Jackson was vicious. And his mind remained a blank.

"Hello."

It was Sara. He took a viciously deep breath.

"Hi," he said, trying to sound as much like his normal self as he could.

"Who is it?" she asked.

He sensed a touch of anxiety in her voice. He had to calm her fears as quickly as possible.

"Jackson."

"Oh," she said.

He'd have to snap back with something attention-getting, something stimulating yet amusing.

"I just called to say" — and here he switched to his best Huck Finn voice — "it ain't proper, Miss Sara, what they doin' to the book. It's downright ignorant, that's what it is."

It was another moment of brilliance, he knew, a gem of an off-the-cuff remark that could only command respect for the quickness of his wit.

She laughed. He loved how her laughter sounded so genuine, how it seemed to brim with admiration.

"How long have you been practicing that?" She laughed again.

He could hardly deny her the moment. She was having such fun.

"Let's get serious now." Rather than let her dwell on his wit, he thought he would score again, this time by going straight to the heart of the matter. "Sara, we've got to do something about this. It's an attack on the very foundations of democracy. It cuts squarely into the meaning of freedom."

She was impressed. She had to be. And the silence at the other end was the proof.

"Jackson," she said, "I didn't know you were so . . . so . . ."

Say it, Sara, say it, he urged in silence.

"So . . . I don't know what the word is."

"Compatible."

She laughed again. God, he loved that laugh. It was so expressive.

There was quiet for a few moments, long enough for him to realize just how eagerly she was anticipating what he would say next.

"Can't we do something about it?" he said.

"There's a meeting Thursday night. It's a public forum to discuss the issue, before the school board votes on whether to remove the book from the reading list."

"What's the plan of attack?" he said aggressively.

"I'm going to speak. And so are a few others. Maybe Adam."

Maybe is right. That mouse didn't have guts enough to argue his way out of a brown paper wrapper. And he would have told her pretty quick, too, except he hardly had the nerve to come on so strong right at that moment.

"Can I depend on you to be there?"

Could she? Did Juliet depend on Romeo? Did Diana depend on Charles?

"Don't even ask," he said. "You can count on me to stand up and give them all I got."

"Come well prepared."

"I always do," he said. "I won't mess up, I promise."

It was a promise he intended to keep. Surely this would be more than enough to win her over.

When he said good-bye to her (cheerfully enough, but with an edge of fierce determination), he could smell victory. It was sweet. Blissfully sweet.

He lay back on his bed and reveled in it.

Now all that remained to be done was figure out what he was going to say Thursday night. It seemed easy enough. The arguments were obvious to anyone who read the book with an open mind. Straightforward, clear, logical. Yet there was a nagging worry — what if the opposition were professionally coached? What if they were better prepared? What if they just looked like they were better prepared? He had seen enough political speeches on TV to know what really mattered. He wondered what image he projected to the public. He wished someone could do a poll on him so he could know how to improve that image.

He needed an edge, a little inside advantage . . .

He took the golden miniature pizza down from his closet. How badly did he want that edge? He knew he *could* take a plunge into the book and see first-hand just what all the fuss was about.

No, it was a dangerous and foolhardy thing to be doing. He

was not yet willing to go to that extreme.

An hour into the meeting on Thursday night and he was thinking that, extreme as it might be, he just might have to do it. Things were not going well for the side opposed to a ban.

It seemed those with the least substance to what they had to say were the ones who spoke the longest and with the most passion. He felt as though he was at a political rally or a convention of sports commentators.

It was all pure emotion. Speakers in favor of a ban cast out lines from the book as if to say the words had only one meaning and it was irrelevant what came before or after or who the character was who said them. Jackson sensed they were people who knew exactly what was wrong with the world and knew exactly how it should be changed and even knew exactly what was going to happen to people who didn't agree with them.

Those who spoke against the ban were just as emotional. They talked of literature as being a window on the real world and how you couldn't ignore history, bad as much of it was. It sounded sensible enough.

Unfortunately, it wasn't sense that most people in the audience seemed to favor. It was something much more fundamental — their own instincts. School, as they saw it, was not the place for anything that might offend anybody. It was as simple as that.

Jackson tried not to be offended. Then he tried being simple-minded. That didn't work either. He knew he would just have to be honest and be himself.

Sara stood up to speak. She said that as a sixteen-year-old she was quite mature enough to be exposed to the foulness of society without embracing it. Most people couldn't tell if she was offending them with that remark and so they ignored her.

Jackson could see that his side was rapidly losing ground. It would take a speech with the passion of a TV evangelist to turn things around for them. With a lot more on his mind than the good of all mankind (namely, the love of a woman), Jackson should have known he could do it if he tried. He just needed the courage.

And a little gold. He put his hand in his pocket and rubbed the pizza medal between his fingers. He stared at his father's gold-edged copy of *The Adventures of Huckleberry Finn* on his lap. He thought of his previous misadventure. He grew faint-hearted.

Then Adam jumped to his feet. Oh man, Jackson thought, and what is the lymph node out to prove now? He's only going to make it worse. And make an even bigger fool of himself in the process.

On second thought, he would resign himself to it. Go for it, Adam. Make my job even tougher. Make me look that much better when I get up to speak.

To Jackson, Adam looked falsely self-assured, too damn falsely self-assured as a matter of fact. What an act — the way he gripped the back of the empty chair in front of him and stared intently at the members of the school board.

"Mr. Chairperson, members of the Board, parents, fellow students," he began. Oh sure, play the sophisticated public speaker for all it's worth. Jackson had heard just about all he could take.

"I think our focus is misplaced here. We must remain rational. We shouldn't get caught up in our emotions and lose sight of the facts."

God, Jackson thought, who fed him those lines? Jackson rolled his eyes. It was pitiful how phony the guy could sound when he put his mind to it.

"The fact is, this book is recognized the world over as a great work of literature. If some of you have a problem with it, then perhaps you are not allowing yourselves to go below the surface and find the true meaning to be found there. Everything might not be as it first appears."

Jackson shook his head. Tell me about it.

"The basis of great art is truth — the world as it is, not as we like to think it is."

You got it, man. Now sit down before you completely blow our credibility.

Adam took his seat. Applause — overly polite, Jackson thought. And the cheers — relatively few. Jackson was sure there was a lack of deep-rooted enthusiasm for what had been said. That had to be obvious to Sara and anyone else with the sense to see beyond the whistling and shouting. Family members, no doubt, scattered about the audience.

Jackson could see him whispering to Sara and smiling. Too damn obviously pleased with himself. The way she took his hand and squeezed it — that Jackson found particularly sickening.

It was a relief to Jackson when he saw her finally come back to her right mind and turn around to him. "You ready?" she asked. "We need the knock-out punch."

Of course, the knock-out punch. The killer stroke of genius that only he could deliver. Her faith was in the right place, he knew, but was it indeed the right moment? Why rush into things? Wouldn't a little longer buildup prove a better strategy?

Then he noticed a gold chain around Sara's neck. It struck him. He had it figured that it must have been the gold in Odysseus's coin that got him out the first time. What if he took the chain with him into *Huck Finn*? He would have a ready means of escape.

It was perfect. A fool-proof insurance policy. He'd stay just long enough to get a feel for the story, and then he'd beat it back and make his pitch to the audience. That really would be perfect timing.

He leaned ahead over Sara's shoulder and in a whisper asked if he could borrow her chain. "I need a good-luck charm. It is real gold, isn't it?"

"Of course it's real gold," Adam said. "Who do you think gave it to her?"

Jackson was tempted to make him look like an even bigger

idiot, but thought better of it, seeing that the poor jerk would soon have his heart broken.

"Jackson," Sara said, "I don't understand."

"Trust me," he replied, firmly but tenderly.

That did the trick. She looked away and removed the chain and passed it to him.

He put it around his own neck. "I'll be right back," he said.

"Where you going?" she asked. He could detect the urgency of having him near her ringing in her voice.

He tried to force a blush. Then he hurried out of the auditorium.

It was the only place he knew for sure he could be private for a few minutes. He sat down on the toilet seat. The sounds of running water made him think of the Mississippi.

He flipped through the book. He knew the part he wanted. It was near the end, where Jim was captured. It was a crowd scene, so Jackson wouldn't be noticed. And it would give him what he was after, he thought — first-hand observation of the hell that was slavery. And when he returned and let loose at the audience with all he had learned from the book, they would be given a picture they wouldn't soon forget. By the time he was finished there wouldn't be a whimper of opposition in the place.

The book open to Chapter 42, he rubbed the fingers of one hand along the golden edges of the paper and the fingers of the other hand against the pizza medal, just as he had done before. Within seconds of starting to read, off he went, of one heart for Sara, indivisible, in the name of liberty and justice for all.

SIX

The timing was excellent. Jackson came to life again in the midst of a crowd, exactly as he had planned. The jostling of bodies, the noise, the general commotion were precisely what he had been counting on. Man, he thought, how good it is to be in such control of your life.

"Nigger, wipe that smile off your face!" some idiot shouted in his direction.

Jackson glanced behind him, to see just who the fool was yelling at, only to get a blob of spit in the face and a clout across the head. He stumbled and fell forward. He tried to catch himself with his hands before he struck the ground, but couldn't. His hands were tied behind his back! He ended up face first in the mud.

"Get up, you stupid ass!" another charmer shouted, together with a few things Jackson had only ever heard at a hockey rink.

Someone pulled him to his feet and then gave him a kick in the backside.

"Who tore off his clothes? Is that what he was wearing underneath?" someone else shouted. "And look what he's got on his feet!" They broke into a wave of howling laughter.

Jackson looked down at himself. He had used his skateboard to get to the meeting; he couldn't have gone dressed any other way. What he was wearing was pink and orange and the sneakers had electric blue bits running through them.

It all looked rather good against black.

Black!

Maybe it was a tan, maybe mud! He looked himself over more closely. Oh shit!

Under other circumstances he wouldn't have minded a color change. He knew being white all the time was a definite disadvantage to anyone like himself who was always on the lookout for injustice in the world.

But not under these circumstances! To go from being a teenager to being a slave was just too brutal a change.

"What's that around his neck?"

"Gold!"

He was lucky to have a neck by the time the hordes retreated. He sank into utter despair. He had no way back. Hell, now what was he going to do?

"Cheer up, Jim," someone whispered to him.

Jim? You mean, he was Nigger Jim?

That's why his hands were tied. Jackson knew he was the most decent character in the whole book. He knew he should have felt proud. But somehow, being not only a slave but a slave who had run away and was now captured, the only thing he could feel was absolutely scared out of his friggin' mind.

"Me and Tom'll get you free ag'in 'fore long, promise," the fellow whispered.

It was Huck. It had to be, even though he didn't look nearly as innocent as he did in the illustrations in the book. Jackson tried to take some heart from Huck's promise. But he knew it wasn't going to be easy. In fact, it was going to be hell.

He wished now that he had never read the book through to the end. Nothing he'd ever done in life could have prepared him for what was to come. He'd had so damn little experience in mass abuse. If he had only known, he could have gone to a few more shopping malls on a Saturday just before Christmas, or worn a cheap brand of sneakers to school.

"Hang the bastard!" someone yelled. And then came a few more graphic descriptions of what some of them might do with knives if they had a chance. "Show all you other niggers what'll happen, in case you get any ideas about runnin' off."

"Now, boys, he ain't ours to hang. What if his owner turns up and finds him at the end of a rope? He'd make us pay for him. Which one of you is goin' to do that?"

Jackson crouched in terror. He knew he wouldn't end up hung — if everything went according to the story. Nevertheless, the spit still dripping from his face was real enough, and there was lots the cheapskates might do to him to make up for the fact they weren't getting the kicks they needed from seeing his sneakered feet dangle above the ground.

They started with a fresh round of cursing, considerably more vivid than anything that had gone before. A few of them took to emphasizing a word or two with cracks about Jackson's head. What he wouldn't have given for a chance back at them! He fantasized about being an uncontrolled Mike Tyson a hundred years into the future.

But his fantasy had precious little time to comfort him. For soon he found himself pushed inside a filthy scrap-lumber cabin, forced into disgustingly rough and poorly designed clothes, and chained to a big iron staple driven into the cabin floor. And, as if that wasn't inhuman enough, they chained together his hands and then both his legs and said bread and water was all he would have to live on. His insides ached with the thought of the hours of suffering that lay ahead. He had never experienced injustice on so severe a scale. He vowed never again to complain about the food in the school cafeteria. Or about how cramped the seating was on airplanes. Or about having to wear clothes that looked brand new.

His captors, zealous louts that they were, gave orders that

two men with guns should guard the cabin every night, and that a bulldog should be tied to the door by day. Great, Jackson thought, that's all I need — some half-starved mutt and a couple of trigger-happy crazies just waiting for some excuse to have at me.

"Don't be no rougher on him than you're obleeged to, because he ain't a bad nigger," someone piped up.

It was the closest thing to a kind word he had heard since he had turned color. He could hardly believe it was directed at him. But he was the one they were all sneering at and cursing when the fellow said it.

And that wasn't all of it. The fellow, who turned out to be a doctor, said not only was Jim not bad, but he had helped save Tom Sawyer's life. Jackson perked up. He knew that had to count for an awful lot, seeing as they had all been going on and on about poor Tom.

Right away they all agreed they would try not to curse the nigger anymore. Jackson moaned. Big deal. He clanged his chains, hoping they might take a hint. No luck. He moved his lips hungrily. Nothing.

"Racist bigots," Jackson grumbled in frustration, unable to keep it in any longer. He peered up at them with a hangdog look, but expecting the worse. They smiled at him as if what he had said was something good to eat.

They all crowded out of the cabin then, without saying much else, appearing reasonably satisfied that they had done the right thing by not hanging him. Huck flashed Jackson a look as he left. It seemed to be a sign for him to keep up his spirits, but even that looked rather half-hearted.

Maybe Huck knew something that he didn't. How much was there about Jim's stay in the cabin that he didn't write down in the book? Was it going to be even more of a hellhole than it looked already?

They shut and barred the cabin door, leaving Jackson in the dark and to his own devices, which weren't many considering the crudeness of the cabin and the radius of the chain from the iron staple in the floor. Within the first few minutes of his imprisonment he had explored pretty well all that there was to explore. He sat down, no more thrilled with the possibility of splinters up his rear from one section of flooring than another.

And the cursed chains. It was going to be a long, cumbersome wait. He clunked them and himself into a prone position, thinking that maybe he'd be able to sleep through most of it. But there was no way that he could get comfortable. Knots in the logs dug at him every way he twisted. His hip and shoulder bones were rubbing through his skin. And he was hard pressed to find an angle for his head that didn't cause him acute pain.

Lying there, he was forced to reflect on just how soft life was for the average North American teenager. It was not something he had ever been inclined to think about before, it not being a very cool thing to do under normal circumstances. Now, though, he had to admit that not being able to buy that leather jacket he tried on in Bloomingdale's shouldn't really have been such a big deal. Or that pair of limited-edition jeans. Or even that greatest hits tape by The Grateful Dead. What he really should have done was count his lucky stars that he had a home and a bed and a flush toilet.

As time wore on and the pressure of his confinement grew, his appreciation for the flush toilet, in particular, soared. In the end he was forced to come to terms with having to live without it.

It was the smell more than anything that he hated. He longed for even the cheapest drugstore fragrance, anything to cloud the air, no matter what shape of bottle it came in. He thought of Sara and how wonderful she smelled and how he would love to be lost in the scent of her close to him. He closed his eyes and let the overwhelming aroma of love take him out of his misery.

Suddenly he smelled a rat! He knew it had to be a rat even though he had never been near one in his life. It was like the smell of a wet hamster in a dirty cage, only stronger. And the scurrying sound. It was all a horrible giveaway.

He dragged himself to his feet as close to instantly as he could, trying to balance himself on the U-shape of the staple and the first few links of the chain. He forced out some rat-terrorizing sounds. The disease-ridden, vermin-infested, rabid little beast scurried away! At least Jackson hoped it was away. He had no way of knowing how far, but he couldn't stay perched where he was forever. All his scare tactics had left him very unbalanced, and he had little choice but to fall back to his feet.

The cabin door opened and in peered two of the most unsightly humans he had ever seen. One carried a lantern, the other a shotgun. They looked possessed of something infectious.

"What's all the commotion in here? You look like you seein' the devil."

"Two," Jackson said. He smiled, relieved that he hadn't completely lost his sense of humor. They stared at him straightfaced, then one looked at the other and grinned, showing a haphazard arrangement of yellowed, broken teeth. The other responded in like fashion.

The pair of dimwits inched closer with the lantern, as if Jackson were a circus animal about to spring at them. When Jackson showed no sign of aggression, one took it into his head to poke at him with the end of his gun. Either the guy's sense of humor was even more primitive than Jackson had estimated, or the fellow was a sadistic jerk anxious for an excuse to do him some damage.

Jackson wasn't about to find out. He concocted the most disgusting images he could and uttered them in a sinister, voodoo-like chant.

"Armpit odor, cigarette-breath,
mucous secretions, slimy and wet;
sight of two nerds, ugly and vile,
festering misfits, hawking bile."

The gruesome pair turned and high-tailed it out of the cabin, cursing Jackson and mumbling something about witches and Satan. It was amazing to Jackson just how quickly they responded to anything that sounded like the work of the devil. He couldn't help but think how many more *Friday the 13ths* there would have been if movies had been invented in that time.

Alone again, he peered into the blackness, but there was no way of telling what and how many hideous, non-human creatures were lurking in the dark crevices of the cabin, all ready to pounce on him as soon as he was asleep. He didn't know what to do. For a long time his mind was at a stand-still.

Finally his indecision got the better of him and he slumped to the floor. He was just too hungry and tired to think straight. He lay there, a listless mound of flesh and bone and chain.

He came to life again when the yelping of a dog outside told him it must be daylight. His eyes made it open after several tries. He untangled himself and got to a position that made him look human.

He was stiff, and full of aches and pains, but, by heaven, his self-respect was still intact. A lesser man would have crumbled under such treatment, he knew, but it was going to take more than a few shackles and bits of iron chain to keep *him* down.

His guts were raging with the fires of injustice and hunger when someone finally showed up with a mug of water and a hunk of stale bread. Just as they'd said they would. Fine with him. He didn't want to be pampered. He didn't want bacon and eggs and toast and coffee and pancakes with syrup or blueberry sauce. He was out to show them he could handle any punishment, no matter how horrible.

The day wore on, and nobody turned up for him to show just how well he was standing up to his ordeal. It was a long and frustrating wait. Finally he sat down again, determined not to sink into any position that would make him look anything but fearless.

Something hissed! He was on his feet, trying to strike a

fearless pose atop the staple and a few links of the chain. He knew what it had to be. He had heard the sound all too often watching reruns of *Mutual of Omaha's Wild Kingdom* on TV. He prayed courageously that it was not the poisonous variety.

A smallish, rather timid-looking snake slithered away in the gloom. To some it might have looked harmless enough, but Jackson had watched enough of those nature-in-the-raw programs to know that such behavior might all be a brilliant evolutionary trick to ensure the survival of the species. He had heard of snakes unlocking their jaws and swallowing eggs. He closed his legs quickly.

He stepped back onto the cabin floor with caution, mindful of the lightning-quick reflexes of animals who feel that someone has invaded their territory. He had no intention of coming out the loser in this deadly game.

"Stay where you are, you slime, if you know what's good for you. Come near me again and you'll have an iron chain wrapped around your friggin' little brain."

Man, it felt good being so tough. He rattled his chains and grunted vigorously.

He stopped when he heard someone outside. He decided maybe it was better to halt his verbal onslaught on the deadly beast. Give it a chance to save some face. If someone showed up to see what all the racket was about, they might just get it into their heads to bring out the whips. Not that he couldn't handle whatever punishment their warped little minds would think up.

He waited and listened. He had never been alone in a room that long without a TV. He had just started to hum a few soft-drink commercials to get himself into a better frame of mind, when he realized that it was Huck's voice he was hearing outside the cabin. Jackson hollered with relief! He shook his chains in restless anticipation of freedom.

Then they burst into the cabin, Huck Finn and Tom Sawyer. It was one of the greatest moments in American literature, and a tremendous relief to Jackson that it happened just as the book said it would.

Huck and Tom had him out of the chains and out into fresh air and sunshine in no time. He had never experienced a greater sense of life and liberty and the pursuit of happiness. It made him swell up with hope that before too long he would actually be able to live the life he wanted to be living.

He still had his pizza medal. It was safely in one of the pockets of his skateboarding clothes, under the rags they had made him put on in the cabin. What he needed now was some other piece of gold. He doubted there was any hope of ever getting back Sara's chain. It was probably holding a locket around the neck of some plantation belle who smelled of magnolia blossoms.

He followed Huck and Tom to the house. All the way they were heaping praise on him for what he had done on the raft. Jackson tried to look the part of the modest hero, but he dared not say anything because he knew for sure he'd never get the accent right.

The best he could do was "yes" and "no," which he figured was safe language for someone used to being a slave. They eyed him a bit strangely, but he took to limping and rubbing his wrists where the shackles had been. That seemed to get them thinking about what a wonderfully good thing they had done for him. There was nothing like boosting people's pride to make them lose their good sense.

At the house he was met by Aunt Polly and Uncle Silas and Aunt Sally. The day before they wouldn't lift a finger to help him, but suddenly now they couldn't give him enough food and drink and pity. They were especially keen on the pity. It seemed to make them feel especially good about themselves.

After an hour Jackson had a gut full and was ready to put his mind to getting out of the mess he was in. He remembered that before long the book was going to end. What would happen if he didn't make it out by then? Would he just end with it, lost in the great void between an author's world and his own, where never the twain shall meet? It had all the dimensions of a sick joke.

But he was sure he remembered something about money in the final couple of pages of the story. Didn't Jim believe for some reason he was rich? It couldn't just have been wishful thinking on Jackson's part.

And then, praying like mad that his memory wasn't faulty, Jackson followed Huck and Tom to a room upstairs. There, like an ending too good to be true, Tom handed him forty dollars. Some of it was gold coin!

"It's for being a prisoner for us the way you was. Go on, take it."

His prayer had been answered. He was delighted beyond words. In fact, he had to literally open his mouth and widen his eyes to keep Tom from being suspicious about why he wasn't saying anything.

At the same time, he was taking a gold coin from Tom's outstretched hand and digging frantically into his clothes to find the pizza medal.

Once he touched it, a current of excitement shot through his body.

"Oh, man!" he burst out, beyond caring what they thought. He could feel his senses melting together and his body drawing away from them.

"Man?" Huck was asking. "What's you sayin', Jim?"

He could barely hear him now, but he did manage a last few words.

"Yeah, dudes, I'm a free man! A free man, man!"

SEVEN

He was back again, back to the washroom cubicle. He felt a terrific sense of relief. And how wonderful to be in the world of modern conveniences. He stood up and admired the thing, then flushed it, delighting in its every gurgle.

He couldn't waste time, though, on past indiscretions. His mind had to be on the present, for his love life stood in the balance.

He threw his hand to his neck. It was there! Sara's gold chain had come back with him. He was amazed, overjoyed, and eternally thankful to whatever had caused it to return.

Book in hand, he unbolted the cubicle door and set forth with newfound confidence, back to the meeting, back to the fight against those who would have Huck and Tom and Jim himself barred from the classroom. It was even more unthinkable now. The attack had become personal. His own pride, black and white, was at stake.

He checked his watch as he ran. Less than five minutes had elapsed. His mind rushed ahead to what he would say. The first rules of effective public speaking were to know your subject and be enthusiastic about it. No sweat. He just hoped his audience played by the rules.

When he entered the auditorium he saw Sara looking over her shoulder to see if he was coming. He cut around the people standing in the back and hurried to his seat.

"They're just about to take the vote," she said urgently. "Where have you been?"

"Research," he said. He slipped the gold chain from around his neck and handed it to her. "Thanks. Proved to be very attractive."

The room was starting to get noisy, in anticipation of the vote. Jackson was back on his feet in an instant.

The noise level fell dramatically. He glanced around the room. They were all turning their heads in his direction. He searched within himself for the strength to meet such a supreme challenge.

He looked at Sara. She was smiling at him, knowingly.

Adrenalin shot through his veins. It would need to be the speech of his life. The tougher the fight, the sweeter the prize.

"Ladies and gentlemen. Should I not say instead simply: friends? For indeed we must all be friends if we are to leave here tonight satisfied that we have done the right thing for the students of this school."

There was complete silence. Not so much as an unavoidable cough.

"Let me ask a simple, yet very direct, question. Who here has felt the pain and humiliation of slavery? What it is to be cast aside as dirt because of the color of your skin? Who among us?"

He paused for effect. Then he held the book up over his head.

"None of us? Friends, I have. I have been cursed at and shackled with chains and fed only bread and water. For I have read this book. I have taken Huck's story and let the words fill my mind with the shame of slavery. I have been called that word *nigger* because I have felt what Jim felt. The words of Mark Twain have cast me back a hundred years. I am thankful to him for that. For I have no fear of words. What I fear is people who say it is better not to know what the words are. There is no shame in the words. The shame is in the people who would have us believe we must not know the truth about the past . . . or the present."

He looked around the room, trying to make eye contact with as many people as he could. He wanted to drive what he was saying deep into their brains.

"Friends, our world was never perfect. We must know the mistakes of the past if we are to deal intelligently with the present and build a future."

It had been a daring move — trying to sound noble and wise while looking like just an average guy. Some of them were staring at him as if they were wondering if they could trust anyone under thirty, others as if he was a hot young radical, a throwback to a time when they were teenagers. It was dangerous, unpredictable territory. Maybe they weren't ready for his brand of common sense.

"Friends, how will we know how far we can go, if we don't know where we started?"

It was the final Kennedy-like punch. And it worked. Someone cheered, then another, then several more. The cheering grew louder and louder, spreading like a wild and uncontrollable urge to be part of something historic. Soon the room was resounding with applause. He felt like a movie star, a rock star, a sports star, a first-time politician.

He sat down. It had all been slightly overwhelming, but not entirely unexpected. He looked at Sara. She was beaming. He felt proud — of himself, of her, even of Adam for taking it so well. The guy must have known that the odds against him were just too great.

Jackson said nothing, just sat there, a modest touch of a smile on his face. The applause eventually eased, then passed away reluctantly.

A restless silence replaced it. The school board was about to vote. The atmosphere grew noticeably more tense. Once they got to the edges of their seats, nobody moved.

Four in favor, five against! Close, insufferably close, but Huck and Jim were free again!

Those around Jackson descended on him like the masses must have descended on David after he dropped Goliath. It was a moment he would remember forever. He had felled the high and mighty. Proof positive that even the tongue is mightier than the sword.

After much hand slapping and back slapping and general pronouncements like "Way to go, dude," the crowd retreated, leaving Jackson to glory in his success. If only it could have been replayed in slow motion, he thought, so that its full effect could be felt.

But the best was yet to come. As Jackson stood up to leave, his head spinning with confidence, Sara pushed aside her chair and walked toward him. Their eyes met. A smile spread ever so slowly across her face. For him it was magic.

Her lips parted. She hesitated. He could see she was having trouble finding the right words. He smiled as if to say there was no need, he understood. He looked deep into her eyes, then broke into a broad, devilish grin.

It was one of those rare moments he would always recall as being perfect. When the ugliness of the outside world intruded and the spell was broken, he was left with the feeling that his life would never be the same again.

Adam came up to them. "I'm glad it's over," he said.

The poor boy. Jackson had to feel sorry for him. He stood there, oblivious to the emotions swirling in the air all about them. Such innocence. One could only wish that the pain wouldn't be too much for him to bear when he finally realized that it was all over between him and Sara. Undoubtedly and absolutely over.

Jackson let them leave together, just the two of them. He felt it was the least he could do. He would call Sara later. He just hoped she would be able do deal with the nasty bit of business all by herself.

He couldn't wait to get home and tell his mother about the

meeting. He couldn't wait to see the look of admiration on her face.

When he got in the house, it was empty. It was an odd emptiness. It was the same emptiness he had felt nine years before when his only goldfish died. He suddenly felt forlorn.

He feared the worst — a final eruption between his mother and his father, with her storming out of the house. It was all he could do to keep from searching the intimate reaches of her room to see what was missing. In the bathroom he did find several expensive-looking cosmetic items with labels written only in French. There was hope.

He sat in the gloom in the living room near the unlit fireplace, full of anxiety. His elation of a short half hour before had been swept away, replaced with a desperate uneasiness about who would be coming next through the front door and what they would be saying.

An hour later, Jackson was still sitting there. It had not been an entirely worry-filled wait. Thoughts of Sara had filled his head for the better part of the time. And then he had taken to reaching up to his father's gold-edged books and taking some of them down.

He had examined each one briefly, before replacing it and taking down another. What he was looking for he wasn't sure. Maybe it was reassurance that no matter how awful his life became there was always an escape at his fingertips. With none of the lineups at airports. He had smiled at his good fortune and returned *Lady Chatterley's Lover* to the shelf.

The front door opened. He drew in his breath heavily. The time it took for whoever it was to come up the stairs seemed endless. The person switched off one light before switching on another. It had to be his father. He was the only one who cared that much about the cost of electricity.

"We're having problems with the new Thanksgiving Turkey Dinner concept," he called out. "It won't fit into most microwaves. The meeting went on forever."

It was music to Jackson's ears. They were still together.

Jackson was rarely in the house alone with his father. He felt a sudden urge to do something warm, and kind, and generous. It was a genuine loving response on his part. But it would also be a good way to see for himself whether there had been any change in his father at all, or if he was still the same self-centred oddity he had known and tolerated all these years.

In distinctly affectionate tones he called out, "Dad."

"Is that you, Jackson?"

Jackson ignored the possibility that another child might have come into their family since that morning. He replied cheerfully, "Yes, Dad."

They met on neutral ground, the hallway outside the bathroom. There was an awkward few seconds as each adjusted to the fact that the other wasn't going anywhere in particular.

Then Jackson came out with it. "Dad, let's make a meal together."

He said it without hesitation, in fact without a thought as to where it had come from. It was his subconscious trying to be heard. His appetite speaking through his heart.

His father looked at him. "Sure," he said. "I guess we'll . . . go for it."

It was said so fondly, so much like they were the kind of father and son who called each other "pal" and went to hockey games together that, for a moment, Jackson was seized with that rock-hard, arm-around-the-shoulder kind of love that he had longed for since he was old enough to play organized sports.

Jackson took off to the grocery store before his father changed his mind. When he returned his father was in the kitchen. For a few minutes there was something unspoken between them that Jackson had never remembered feeling before. He had never treasured silence so much in his life.

They started with a salad. It was a simple lettuce, tomato and cucumber salad with a few sliced mushrooms thrown over the top, but somehow in the slicing and the tearing of the ingredients there developed a camaraderie that was the stuff of which poignant movies are made.

"Dad, where did you learn to slice like that? You're a real artist."

"You mean it?"

"Sure I mean it."

"I wish your mother could see that."

There was a silence, of a different type, that lingered, threatening to turn awkward. Jackson waited; his father coughed. Yet Jackson knew he had struck on something that he couldn't let pass unprobed.

"She didn't appreciate your salads?" Jackson hoped it was enough.

"I'm sure she thought her own artistic aspirations were more important than anything I could ever do with food."

"Really?" Had his father exposed a root of his discontent?

His father's silence returned, more threatening than ever. And he suddenly seemed to be losing interest in the salad they were making. Jackson knew he would have to change the subject or risk losing everything that had built up between them.

"Ah, what the hell, let's have steak with it."

"What?"

"Those moose steaks in the freezer downstairs, the ones Uncle Winse brought."

"All that red meat . . ."

Jackson thought a lot of his Uncle Winston, the wildlife officer, who always brought some sort of wild game whenever he visited from Newfoundland. He was so down to earth.

Jackson could see his father still hesitating. "C'mon, Dad."

It was amazing — his father's face suddenly broke into a grin of sorts and he said, "Ah, what the hell."

Jackson could hardly believe it. He was beside himself with anticipation of what might come next.

His father let out a short but uncontrolled laugh.

Jackson laughed too.

And then his father let go again. This time longer and even less controlled.

And it grew and grew, until it seemed both of them were having such a good time that Jackson thought nothing would ever be the same between them again.

But then, as quickly as it had come, it was gone.

Katherine came back from wherever she had been. She looked in the kitchen.

"There's lots," Jackson said.

She glared at the two of them. "Forget it."

As soon as she left his father took several mouthfuls of salad and began to talk about the need to curb inflation and how one had to plan carefully for retirement.

It was painful to see the snap back to his old ways.

Over the moose steak, his father grew depressingly serious. He began talking of the reliability records of North American–made cars and the merits of lap-top computers.

Neither of them finished their meals.

Jackson couldn't believe it had come to this. He couldn't believe that his mother's presence alone could cause such a drastic change in his father's behavior. Maybe she brought with her an overabundance of the wrong kind of ions, or maybe the chemical content of her make-up was causing a new and strange type of allergic reaction. Maybe it was the first case of some twenty-first-century disease.

Whatever it was, his father's new spirit of cooperation was gone without a trace. He was back to being just as self-absorbed and inflexible as he had ever been.

There was, however, cause for hope. Jackson knew now that his father was at least capable of changing.

That did something to make up for the fact that he was the one left to clean up the kitchen. His father had abandoned it as if he had been caught in enemy territory and his mother was nowhere to be seen. Jackson stood there with a full stomach but an empty heart. It put him in no mood to work at getting the burnt-on bits off a greasy frypan.

But get them off he did. Out of disgust, more than anything. With every squirt of detergent his anger grew. In the end the kitchen was even cleaner than it was before the meal. But it was a vengeful, unloving cleanliness.

Hands wrinkled and smelling of lemon freshness, he went in search of his mother. He found her upstairs, behind a closed door, manicuring her nails. It was adding insult to injury.

He held out his soggy hands. "Here," he proclaimed. "Satisfied?"

She didn't bat a mascaraed eyelash.

He groaned his disgust.

She looked up. "It's your father you should be looking for sympathy from, not me."

"It's not sympathy I'm looking for."

"What is it, then? Praise? For doing something I've been doing every evening for the last ten years while your father watched TV or played with his computer?"

"You're mad because we were having a meal together."

"I might be, but that's got nothing to do with it."

"Oh, sure."

"It's true. Even though it was a rotten thing for you to be doing. I thought we had an agreement."

"We do. It was only an experiment, to see how he would react."

"And what did this little experiment prove — that he loves to eat but hates cleaning up?"

"What it proved is that he can be different, he can change. I saw it happen, right before my very eyes."

"I find that hard to believe."

"It's true."

"And what brought about this sudden rehabilitation?"

"I don't know."

"And what snapped him out of it?"

"I'm not sure of that either."

"Easy come, easy go."

"Now you're being facetious."

He loved it when he could use one of his mother's favorite words to his own advantage. It brought her back to reality. He wasn't just some teenage subspecies whose body was maturing at a faster rate than his brain.

"Are you sure there's not something you two need to work out?" he said, not without a certain amount of anger. "Like, from the past, maybe."

"Like what?"

"I dunno. The relationship of what we eat to our artistic urges?"

"Did he say that?"

"I'm not sure."

"If he's got something to say, let him say it to me," she snapped. "Meanwhile the clock keeps ticking. One week and counting."

"You're not still planning to leave? Seriously?"

She wasn't smiling.

His heart sank. In seven days he could be packing up and leaving what had been his home all these years, heading off to some rathole of an apartment in god knows what part of town.

It was all too much for him. He had to get out of the house and seek some consolation somewhere.

EIGHT

His mother let him borrow the car without any preconditions other than the ones he had agreed to before they let him have his license — no drinking, no drugs, no smoking, no speeding, no more passengers than the number of seatbelts, no unbecoming behavior. At times she also threw in no eating of anything that might stain or leave a smell, but tonight she was being liberal.

He drove around for a while, slowing down as he went by Masterpizza. Then he tore off down the strip of neon hamburgers and revolving chicken buckets, past other places with more subdued signs but better ads on TV. Right to the end and in a full circle through the parking lots of Greenacres Mall, and then back up the strip again. It was just what he needed — reassurance that there was stability in the world, that if all else failed him the straightforward, everyday, all-out world of fast food and shopping malls would always be there, eager to make him happy. He smiled to himself just like people did in mouthwash commercials.

There was only one thing missing. A girl beside him in the car.

And there was only one way to remedy that situation. He stopped by a phone booth and dialed Sara's number. He did it with all the confidence in the world. There was no lingering doubt, no last-minute regret that the thrill of the chase was over.

"Hello?"

"Hi. It's Jackson." There was a distinct note of victory in his voice.

"Oh. Hi." Did he detect an attempt to fake surprise?

He laughed aloud. It was a hearty, playful laugh. "Can't we get together tonight? I'm dying to see you."

So bold, yet so truthful. He felt as though it was the beginning of a new era in his relationships with the opposite sex.

"We should. There's something I have to tell you."

God, was he ready for this — his most fervent dreams coming true? He braced himself with one hand against the side of the telephone booth. He was weak with fulfillment.

"I have a car," he said, his head spinning.

"I'll be waiting for you."

They each said a hesitant good-bye and Jackson let the receiver slip through his hand, back to its place.

He let loose with a yell, full of all the good things about being young, and male, and in love.

He wasted no time getting to Sara's house. Actually he got there so quickly that he drove past it — he knew it wasn't good for anyone his age to appear too eager about anything, no matter how badly he wanted it. He wasted several extra minutes before returning and pulling into the driveway.

He ignored the doorbell in favor of a more rugged, virile approach. He knocked with a heavy yet rhythmic knock, then checked that the collar of his jacket was turned up. If there had been something to lean his shoulder against, he would have leaned.

She came to the door dressed and ready to go. He was hoping for an invitation inside, but she was obviously just as eager as he was for them to be alone.

"Where will we go?" he said with a smile that he could

barely keep under control. It was their first date. He wanted it to be some place special.

"Somewhere quiet, a place we can talk." That really cut down on their choices. There were some parking spots he knew about, but he couldn't be that optimistic.

"I know," he said, "that new place, Canucks."

"The 'genuine Canadian home-style burger' place?"

"Yeah, it's never crowded. But I hear their Mountieburger is great. It's made with backbacon and a secret sauce. And they also have Prairie chicken nuggets with real maple syrup to dip them in."

"I'm not hungry."

"Me neither. But I could use an ice-cold mug of Moose Milk."

They soon found themselves in a good imitation of a log cabin, drinking brownish milkshakes from mugs shaped like moose heads, and munching on something called Beaver Chips.

They looked at each other across a corner table made of roughly hewn birch. There was the glow of a real firelog in a real fireplace. The atmosphere was close to perfect — intimate, yet with the raw touch of nature.

She was less talkative than he had expected. Like him, she probably needed some time to adjust, time to let the wonder of it all sink in. He was content to just sit there and let himself be excited by how beautiful she was. A tough fight it had been, but how awesomely sweet the prize!

After a while she seemed to have found the right words to fully express what she was feeling. She was naturally nervous. He knew that was as it should be. Words from the heart never come easy.

"Jackson," she said. He had never heard his name spoken so tenderly before.

He wanted to make it easier for her. "Yeah."

"I really like you . . ."

She was pausing. The tension was killing him. And . . .

"But . . ."

But! It was like a knife-point in his chest.

"I have to be honest . . ."

Honest?

"I'm just not ready to break up with Adam."

Shock. Disbelief. Severe discontent.

"I mean, you're a great guy, and it was really wonderful what you did at the meeting, but . . ."

He didn't think he could handle another *but*. His head snapped to one side. He had been wounded and it hurt. He had to get to the heart of the matter.

"What the hell's he got that I haven't?"

"It's not that simple."

"I can take it. Go ahead, hit me again."

"I like him a lot, that's all."

"More than you like me."

He waited. She didn't say anything. He knew it — she didn't say anything because she couldn't bring herself to lie.

Man, he couldn't believe it! That Adam had her brainwashed, her common sense muzzled, her self-image ruined! What could he do? What would it take for her to realize just what the guy had done to her? He decided the only approach was to confront her squarely with the truth, shock her into seeing just how great they could be together.

"Sara, I love you. It's a fact."

Her cheeks glowed with the fire. She closed her eyes, like her head was reeling from the impact.

It was a cruel favor he was doing her, but he knew it would only be a matter of time before she would be thanking him for it.

"Jackson," she said, "I don't know how to say this."

"Let me count the ways."

"Jackson!" There was a sharpness in her voice.

He felt real pain. It hurt and there was no hiding it.

Then she laughed. Just quietly at first, then much, much louder.

"Oh, Jackson."

He laughed too. It had been like living through a natural disaster.

"You're such a character." She laughed again.

He loved it.

"How can I not like you?"

More, more.

"But . . ."

"Dammit, Sara, give it a chance!" he exploded. "When was the last time you and Adam had a genuine, spontaneous laugh together?"

That got to her, that really got to her.

"Aren't you ready for a little craziness in a relationship? I can be cool, but I can also be lots of fun."

That started her gray matter stirring in new and unpredictable ways. She looked at him without blinking.

"Together we could really be something different," he said, anxious to add fuel to that spark he was sure he saw in her eyes.

"Jackson, I don't know . . ."

It was a start. He grabbed onto it.

"You'll never know until you give it a try. You can't go through life wondering how great it could have been."

"I'll think about it. I think we should go."

Not good.

He had tried every technique he knew, short of threatening to do himself physical damage. He had ruled that out from the very beginning. He was never big on self-inflicted pain, particularly when there was no guarantee it would have the desired effect.

Surely there was some way through to her heart. All the while in the car back to her house he tried as hard as he could to come up with some wildly romantic phrase that would do it for him. Nothing. His mind was a hopeless blank.

When he pulled into the driveway it was with the feeling that the only chance he would have would be to make one last, desperate move.

"Sara, I have to see you again."

"I'll call you."

Her voice had a rather dull ring to it.

"I'll be holding my breath," he said.

"It can't be that bad." She laughed.

Not such a terrific joke, but he loved her for it. She got out of the car and closed the door. When she reached her front door, she looked back at him. It was not the look of relief he was dreading. He was out of the car and by her side in seconds. He smiled, trying not to beam.

"Jackson, you're no Romeo, but you're sweet."

Sweet. He gritted his teeth.

Suddenly, his eyes bulged as if his head couldn't hold the swell of inspiration that had mushroomed inside.

No, it couldn't work — could it?

Sara turned to go inside. He caught a glimpse of the gold chain around her neck.

"Wait!"

She turned.

"Wait. Wait right there. I'll be right back."

He ran to the car and jumped inside. He drove the gear stick into reverse, checked for traffic, and, whipping out of the driveway, he took off down the street.

He made it to his house in minutes, having carefully avoided the crowds just getting out of the Bingo Palace. He left the car running and rushed into the house. He headed straight to the living room. His eyes swept the bookshelf until he came to Shakespeare. He fingered past each thin volume until he found it — *Romeo and Juliet*.

As he turned to leave, he saw his father, newspaper in his hands, looking at him from a chair on the other side of the room. He had been caught red-handed.

"So," his father said.

"And?" Jackson replied.

"And so it wasn't just your mother who's been fooling up

the books."

"The books are not what's fooled up! Dad, they're not sacred idols you've got there. And just because they're not on the best-seller list anymore doesn't mean they can't be opened up and read and lived with and talked about. It's Van Goghs and Picassos you've got to keep in mint condition, not books."

His father seemed too stunned to answer him. He hadn't meant to sound like a know-it-all, but he knew it was hard not to, given the state of his father's mind.

He left the room and raced up the stairs to his bedroom. There he uncovered the pizza medal, replaced its companions once again, and raced back down the stairs. He passed his mother on his way out the door.

"I don't think I'm in any hurry for the car," she said. She must have overheard the encounter with his father.

He was back on the street and on his way to Sara's as quickly as possible. Showing great restraint, he stayed within the speed limit and didn't curse a single red light.

He pulled into her driveway. She was sitting on her front step. He sat down next to her. She clearly needed an explanation for this rather curious departure from the usual good-night kiss.

"I have something for us to do together. It's sort of a ritual."

She drew away from him.

"No, really, it's okay. See this book?"

"*Romeo and Juliet.*"

"Remember in the school play . . . the balcony scene?"

She nodded, her doubts intensifying.

"Remember your lines? Here they are." He had found the page, the beginning of Act Two, Scene Two.

"Do you always do this when you take out a girl for the first time?"

"Trust me. It'll be a very moving experience for you." He smiled.

She didn't.

He placed the pizza medal on the book. "Now, see this . . .

it's gold. And see the gold on the edge of the pages?"

"What is it?" she said, staring at the medal.

"Pizza."

Her eyes moved about in funny, confused ways.

He pushed on. "Now, follow what I'm doing."

He held half the medal with two fingers of his right hand, then she held the other half with two fingers of her left. He began rubbing the gold edge of the paper with the fingertips of his other hand. She did the same.

A cold look of irritation was just beginning to form on her face when suddenly her expression changed. She looked at Jackson, a lovely, carefree smile on her lips.

There was no resisting them. Their lips met and in an instant they were off, transported by the awesome mixture of love, gold and the written word.

NINE

For Jackson it was a dream, a wild and extraordinary dream come true. Their lives recast, he and Sara awoke as the most famous pair of young lovers the world has ever known. It increased his appreciation of Shakespeare a thousandfold.

Here he was in among the shrubs of a lush garden in fifteenth-century Italy and looking up at the famed stone balcony. And there on that balcony, aglow with light from a yonder window, was his fair Sara. Fair and glowing, but quite bewildered, despite her made-in-Italy Benetton top. He would have to act quickly if he was going to make her think it was a dream she was having about the school play.

"But, soft! what light through yonder window breaks?" he whispered loud enough for her to hear.

It worked. She suddenly fell into her role, like someone not wanting to make a fool of herself in front of an audience. Her face saddened, in longing for her lover. It was wonderful to see. He loved being longed for.

She leaned her cheek against her hand. And waited. He stared, entranced by her longing. She continued to wait. How long? Her longing was beginning to look painful.

He snapped to his senses. "O! that I were a glove upon that

hand, / That I might touch that cheek."

"Ay me!" she sighed. He thought it such a marvelous, love-sick sigh.

"She speaks. O, speak again, bright angel . . . "And a lot more that he stumbled over. Something about a winged messenger of heaven. It was so hard to remember the less famous lines when all he could really concentrate on was Sara. ". . . And sails upon the bosom of the air." At least he got the last line right.

"O Romeo, Romeo! wherefore art thou Romeo?" He had never heard the words spoken with more passion. It was all he could do to hold himself back and not burst out with an answer.

He restrained himself against the wall and let her timeless words swell his heart.

"What's in a name? That which we call a rose / By any other name would smell as sweet."

How true, he thought, how true. Romeo? Jackson? What's in a name?

He jumped forth and called up to her in all his eagerness. "I take thee at thy word: / Call me but love, and I'll be new baptiz'd; / Henceforth I never will be Romeo."

There could be no mistaking his love for her. But still he was in the dark as far as she was concerned. It wasn't in the play for her to see him yet. What he didn't have to suffer in the name of a good script!

"What man art thou, that, thus bescreen'd in night, / So stumblest on my counsel?"

His admiration for Sara swelled even more. *Bescreen'd* was such an awkward word. And *stumblest* was another mouthful. He had to admire Shakespeare too. The man must have written all those plays without a thesaurus.

And so Jackson stumbled right along. "My name, dear saint, is hateful to myself . . . Had I it written, I would tear the word." He put an extra emphasis on *tear*. He figured it added a little of his own natural toughness to the character.

Jackson could hardly wait for the next part. He braced himself for the big revelation. Now she would see that there was more behind that voice than a good set of vocal cords.

"Art thou not Romeo, and a Montague?"

"Neither, fair maid, if thee dislike."

And then out from the shadows he came! Her eyes fell on him. It was, of course, a bit startling to her to find it wasn't Adam. Mouth slightly agape, eyebrows tightened, a momentary loss of breath — none of it was unexpected. Jackson smiled dreamily, and in time Sara realized there was a new Romeo in her life.

He sensed a certain freshness in her voice, a delightful intensity that wasn't there before. "How cam'st thou hither, tell me, and wherefore?"

He was quick to respond, and with all the passion he dared display. "With love's light wings did I o'erperch these walls . . . thy kinsmen are no stop to me."

"If they do see thee, they will murder thee."

He found it amazing what he had done for her acting. The *murder* came out wonderfully strong. His sudden appearance had really unleashed her talent.

But then it was his turn to impress her. The fearlessness of his love had to speak louder than even Shakespeare's words. "Alack!" He tried to make it sound like he was swearing, so his speech would have a more modern feel to it. "There lies more peril in thine eye / Than twenty of their swords . . ."

It was asking a lot, he knew, but he hoped she could get the deeper message in that line — not only would he be undaunted in his pursuit of her, but that it was Adam who was the real enemy.

He gave her time. She spoke on and on, mere lines of a play. But gradually, as her dialogue grew longer and his love more unswerving, he was sure he detected a mellowing in her voice. Then a sense of daring. And then gradually something not unlike wild abandon.

He could see it wasn't just good acting. He could see she

was finally breaking free of the dullness that was Adam and stretching out for some fresh, new excitement in her life.

His heart soared. It was the moment he had been waiting for, and he was determined to make the most of it. "Lady, by yonder blessed moon I vow . . ."

"O, swear not by the moon . . .," she said, with a smile he was sure was meant only for him.

"What shall I swear by?" he answered, venturing a quiet but carefree laugh.

He saw it as a game now, this dialogue. The lines were thrown back and forth, each more charged than the one before it with the undercurrent of their love.

"O, wilt thou leave me so unsatisfied?" he said, a glint in his eyes.

"What satisfaction canst thou have to-night?" she answered, not without a certain caution in her voice against letting his imagination get carried away.

"Th' exchange of thy love's faithful vow for mine."

The plea for commitment was staring her in the face. This was the true test. Was she really willing to cast aside Adam for him? He waited, his breathing suspended.

When she spoke, it was like an answer from heaven, spoken, he knew, with the sincerity of an angel. "My bounty is as boundless as the sea, / My love as deep: the more I give to thee, / The more I have, for both are infinite."

He was weak with ecstasy. It was the closest he had ever come to breaking out spontaneously in Elizabethan song.

The Nurse called to her from inside the house. As Juliet turned and glanced at him, she put her hands to her neck and undid the gold chain, that last earthly reminder of Adam. She drew her hand delicately back, and then threw it as hard, Jackson thought, as if she were ridding herself of the devil.

She disappeared inside, just missing Jackson's quick loss of ecstasy.

The chain arced through the air, glinting in the moonlight, flaunting its power over him.

Jackson backed up, all the time trying to keep his eye on the chain. He was like some outfielder desperate to prove he was worth his astronomical salary.

He went back, back, back to the orchard wall, then leapt into the air, his hand outstretched.

He caught it, a perfect one-handed catch!

The crowd roared. Then unsheathed their swords. Jackson looked up. Oh no! Not Capulets guarding the orchard wall!

He ran as fast as he could toward the balcony, the chain in one hand, his other hand digging out the pizza medal from his pocket, and the Capulets in pursuit. Sara had just reappeared after her visit with the Nurse. The encounter seemed to have left her in a state of shock.

There was a vine-covered trellis below the balcony, just as all the set designers said there should be. He climbed it frantically. Sara leaned over the railing.

"Juliet," he called. "Juliet, give me thy hand!" Too disoriented to realize that the line wasn't in the play, she did as he asked.

He grasped the back of her hand with his, then put the chain and the pizza medal in her palm and locked his other hand over it.

He rubbed their palms together. He could feel a lightness overcoming him. Not a minute too soon. He glanced over his shoulder. The guards were almost at his heels, but they were fading fast . . .

"Good night, good night! parting is such sweet sorrow," his Juliet was heard to utter, as together they began their long and rapturous journey home.

TEN

It had been a short but phenomenal trip. Their lips had not parted. In fact, when Jackson opened his eyes and discovered what he was enjoying so much, he went at it with renewed interest.

That brought a cheer from the sidewalk. It startled Sara into tearing herself apart from him. Stopped on the sidewalk in front of the house were several kids on bicycles. One was holding a watch in his hand.

"Four minutes, thirty-four seconds!"

"Don't you guys' lips get tired?" said another.

Jackson told them to get lost, and they quickly rode off, more confused than ever about what was going to happen to them when they reached adolescence.

Sara was on her feet, embarrassed, and, understandably, somewhat bewildered. Yet Jackson was sure she was no longer the distant would-be girlfriend. Four and a half minutes was surely proof positive of compatibility.

"Jackson," she said, "I've never been kissed like that in my life. It was . . ."

He couldn't resist. "Out of this world."

"Unreal."

She looked at him. Wasn't it the same look she had given her Romeo? Jackson was sure it was. He was immensely relieved. Her love for him had withstood the test of time.

"I better go in."

He fully appreciated that it couldn't go on all night.

"Will I see you again?" she asked.

His delight in it all surged through his body yet again. "By the hour of nine," he said, laughing heartily, now her true Romeo.

She smiled, then broke into laughter with him. "'Tis twenty years till then," she said, his Juliet, he just knew it, now and forever.

She leaned over and gave him a quick kiss, again on the lips. Then she disappeared inside.

He was left to lean limp against the house, his body filled to overflowing with love's sweet, sweet juices.

His taste for girls had finally been satisfied. All the way home he could think of nothing except Sara and how glad he was that he had kept his appetite for the opposite sex in check until he'd won the heart of the girl he really wanted. His mind feasted on the great times ahead for the two of them.

All that thinking was making him very hungry, and once through the door he headed straight for the kitchen and made himself a snack of the leftover moose. He had it half gone before he sensed that something might be drastically wrong.

He walked reluctantly out of the kitchen, chewing a last piece of meat. He walked about downstairs, looking into rooms and finding them empty. He went upstairs, but failed to find anyone there either. What he did find was evidence of a hasty departure by his mother — drawers half open and near empty, a closet bare of clothes except for a yellow polyester pantsuit she had kept as a reminder of carefree, happier days. Her jewelry box, her unopened bottle of Obsession, her copy of *Our Bodies, Ourselves,* all gone. It was a sad and depressing sight.

In his room he found a note from her. It said simply: "I'm gone to find us a place. I'll be coming to get you early in the morning. Love, Kath(erine)."

He tried to read more into the note, but it proved to be a meaningless search. Tears came to his eyes. There was no holding them back. He had gone from the heights of ecstasy to the depths of melancholy twice in one evening. As an adolescent he had experienced plenty of mood swings, but this was just too much. He lay down on his bed and started to feel intensely sorry for himself.

He fell asleep and dreamed it had all been a bad dream and that his parents were actually downstairs in the kitchen eating wild rice together and listening to Jim Morrison's version of "Light My Fire."

What woke him was the sound of a smoke detector. He jumped to his feet and rushed down the stairs into the kitchen.

There was only one person there — his father. He was eating what looked like burnt multi-grain toast.

Jackson didn't know what to say to him. He could have vented his frustration with some cutting and vengeful remark. He could have told him how dated his haircut was. There was no end to the insults he could have hurled at him.

Instead, all that would come out was, "She's gone?"

"It wasn't all my fault," his father said.

Maybe so, but the man was a fool. And what was worse, he was a stubborn fool. And he looked beyond any help, like there was no possible way that he could ever be made to see the light. Maybe he should just have been left to suffer all the misery that was due him.

When Jackson looked at his father, though, he knew he could never bring himself to let him suffer in that way. The man was his father, after all. And there flowed in their veins a concern for each other that went beyond such cold-hearted logic.

No, there would be no messy scene where the son vows never to do anything for the father ever again. And then packs his things and leaves the father to withdraw broken-hearted into himself, there to live out his life in utter despair, a victim of his own selfishness. No, he was only content to let his father suffer through his burnt bread.

Jackson left the kitchen. He plodded upstairs to his room, his body heavy with the strain he felt from showing so much restraint.

He sat on his bed, adrift, seeking comfort where he could. Even Gauguin's girls seemed distant, less spellbinding. His mind darted about in all directions in an effort to find something that would relieve his anxiety. He considered phoning Sara, but he thought it better not to burden her with his troubles while she was probably, right at that moment, in the middle of untangling herself from Adam. He thought of resorting to foreign substances, but he decided that was too easy a way out. He dismissed a little sexual diversion out of hand as too simplistic and short-term a solution.

In the end he left the house, with the hope that he would at least be able to look at things more objectively. He wandered aimlessly, through streets where the only things stirring were ugly dogs who stopped barking as soon as he swore at them. He passed house after house, each no doubt filled with people enjoying uncomplicated lives. The hum of the streetlights mixed with the faint sounds of happy families listening to Anne Murray.

He was hoping for something to calm his nerves. Instead, his walk was leaving him more rattled than ever. He made a quick detour to the fast-food strip. There, in the unending glare of its lights, he thought for sure he would find the comfort he was seeking. He would feel wanted, needed. It would be tremendous value for his money.

He headed straight for Masterpizza, only to discover it closed. He cupped his hands to his face and pressed them against the window. There was not so much as a reading light inside. He would have to tell Mrs. Landsberg that library hours just weren't going to work in the business world.

He went back up the street to McDonald's. For the cost of fries and a burger and a medium drink he tried again to feel part of something warm and loving. He wanted to be just like the people in the commercials — one of the crowd, yet special. It didn't work. He decided he would have to order a sundae and try harder.

A few students from his classes were there — late-night lovers holding hands dreamily over trays empty except for tracings of ketchup and unopened packets of vinegar. They sucked noisily on melted ice without breaking the magic between them. Jackson knew that it was scenes like this that made fast-food eating such a marvelous thing. So why wasn't it working for him, too? Why was it not restoring his faith in the essential goodness of the world?

He ordered another large fries and ate them slowly, one at a time, hoping to savor the goodness he knew had to be there somewhere. Consumer groups had rated these the best of the fast-food french fries. His father had always told him that. Was this his father's ultimate betrayal?

The thought was another emotional blow to add to his list. But what it did was make him even more determined to set things right in his family. He knew if he didn't act — and fast — it would be the permanent end of the three of them as a family unit. Imperfect as it had been at times, he was not willing to give that up without one last all-out effort.

Exactly what kind of all-out effort, he wasn't certain. But he did know it wouldn't be easy. His father's mind was set in concrete, it seemed, and it was going to need a good pounding to loosen it up. He considered several possibilities, but they all seemed to be too reasonable to work. What was needed was something so unsettling, so emotionally disruptive, that it would make him crave the company of his wife. Jackson thought of having him sit through several Joan Rivers comedy routines in a row, but he wasn't sure if anybody would have anything like that on tape.

All the way home, with the lights of the strip receding none too quickly behind him, it became increasingly clear that time was running out. His mother would be coming for him in the morning and then there really wouldn't be any turning back. The time for decision-making was at hand.

But first he would just have to get some sleep. When he arrived home he headed straight for his bedroom. He would get up as early as he could in the morning and decide then what to do.

He undressed, climbed into bed, took a quick look at Gauguin's girls to help stabilize his thought patterns, then turned out the light.

He slept, but not well.

ELEVEN

The last time he woke up the cursed red digits on his clock radio told him that it was still only five in the morning. He decided it would be useless trying to get back to sleep. He had regained enough strength to make up his mind about what to do.

He put on some clothes and went silently down the stairs. The refrigerator hummed like a friend in the night, leading him through the gloom and into the kitchen. He fumbled around for the handle, finally opening the door. He looked inside, and shook his head sadly. Some friend.

He closed the door and walked with a heavy heart into the living room. He turned on the lamp nearest the bookcase. He tried to get as comfortable as he could in his father's chair.

He looked up at the rows of books. They had served him pretty well in the past, all things considered. Maybe there was one among them now that could save him from the fate that was so fast approaching. It was expecting a lot of a book, he realized, to rescue a marriage, especially when it wasn't on any best-seller list or written by some movie star or psychologist.

He went from book to book, considering each in turn. Some he dismissed right away. Others he wasn't sure about, since he had never heard much about them as books, or even as movies.

Still others he fingered thoughtfully but returned to the shelf with regret. After several minutes he was fast coming to the conclusion that the search was a waste of time, time better spent gearing up for separation from the bedroom and its contents that had been the centre of his life all those many years.

He wandered regretfully up the stairs. He agonized.

The faintest traces of his mother's perfume led him to the spare room. He was seeking comfort, and something more, something to put his world back together. At first he felt awkward, an invader of a privacy not meant for a teenage son. But he knew his desperation was justified, and if it led him into the contents of her personal life, then so be it. Love, he understood only too well, knows no bounds.

He poked through drawers that ultimately held clues to nothing except the power of the fashion industry to convince people to buy things that don't look good on them. It was a battered Hush Puppies shoebox that finally gave him real reason to pause.

In it he found photographs, reminders of a more innocent, pre-videocamera era. There were pictures of his parents on the rocky shorelines of Newfoundland, with friends, smiling foolishly around picnic tables lined with beer bottles. And others, with the two of them embracing in the midst of what looked like thousands of people outdoors in the rain watching someone on a stage playing a fiddle. It really did seem like they were having a good time.

And then there were other pictures showing them as proud parents, cuddling the wrinkled bundle that was him, their newborn. Jackson had never seen them looking happier. It put a painfully hard lump in his throat.

But it was not the pictures that ultimately brought him to a standstill. At the bottom of the box was a book. It was covered in paisley fabric and titleless, with only "Classic Beginnings" stamped in small gold letters on a lower corner of the back cover. It was one of those blank books such as he'd seen in gift shops, the kind of shop that had only a few scattered books to dress up the pine furniture.

The pages were no longer all blank, however. And when he started to look through them he recognized the handwriting immediately. The first entry was dated several months before he was born. He flicked through the pages to the final entry — the day of his birth.

He turned back quickly to the first page. The words of the opening line swelled up at him. "I'm going to have a baby!!" it exclaimed. "I can't believe it . . . so quickly, after all those years on the pill." He stopped, somewhat taken aback, thinking how much older he might have been had they not used birth control. Or how he might not have been at all if they had not stopped.

He read on, without any preconceptions of what else he might find. "I think it's going to be a Jack. John thinks it's going to be a Jacqueline." He knew it. He had started off on the wrong foot with his father even before he had any.

"We will both love it dearly, whatever it is." Jackson was relieved, despite the thought of being neutered.

He was fascinated with all his mother wrote over the months leading up to the big day when he finally got to be born. It had all the ingredients of a best-seller — sex, extreme tension, overblown characters. And a truly happy ending. In fact, it was the final few lines that most intrigued him.

"We are both amazed that we have produced such a dear, sweet son. We're sure he'll grow up to be truly original. John has made a fabulous meal for the two of us in celebration. It is the happiest day of our life together. We wish we could relive it again."

Jackson's eyes filled with water. He read the words over and over. The lump had returned to his throat, harder than ever.

Suddenly, through all that emotion, a path cleared to his brain. He realized he might have found what he had been looking for. If he could make it work his parents *would* relive that great moment. They *would* get a second chance at the happiest day of their life together. Maybe then they would see what it was that made them a family.

There were no gold edges to the paper, but there was that gold imprint on the back cover. It was worth a try. Whatever the consequences, it had to be better than just lying about waiting for the final family disintegration. Where before there was despair, now there was hope. Where there was fear of divorce, now, suddenly, there was the possibility of his getting back to New York.

But first things first. He would have to plan things carefully. He went silently to his bedroom. There he worked on his strategy, sitting at his desk with a quilt bundled around him. It would be a risky piece of business, but, thinking about the results of his escapade with Sara, he knew he was certainly up for it.

An hour later, when he was sure he could smell his father's All-Natural Cream of Oats 'n Bran, he made his way downstairs and walked quietly into the kitchen. His father looked up from his bowl of cereal.

"So, Dad, what do you make of the price of gold these days?" Jackson said, and sat down next to him.

It caught him off guard, but his father was quick to pick up on any interest his son might have in the world of finance.

"Up to 385.25 U.S. an ounce. Might go higher. Hard to predict."

"Dad, what say we go for the gold, so to speak."

"What are you talking about, Jackson?"

"You know — buy an ounce or something."

"You mean buy a gold coin . . . as an investment?"

"Exactly."

"Not on your life."

"Why not?"

"Well, for a start, you don't have that kind of money. And besides . . . Let's just say, gold is unpredictable."

That hesitation had the silence of a bad experience to it. Jackson grabbed at it. "You mean it backfired on you once before?"

His father hesitated again.

"You mean you had a gold coin . . . ?"

"Several."

"You mean you owned several gold coins and when you sold them the price of gold had gone down?"

"Not exactly."

"What, then?"

"I still have the gold."

"You what?" Jackson could not believe his good fortune.

"I have the gold, but not the coins." He held out his left hand. "This wedding ring is 91.7 percent gold."

"Really? I naturally assumed . . ."

"I had some coins before we were married, old Newfoundland two-dollar gold pieces my father kept when Newfoundland joined up with Canada in 1949."

"Wow," Jackson said quietly.

"When we decided to get married, I had those coins melted down and made into rings. It was all very symbolic."

"I can imagine."

"The price of gold went sky-high days after we said 'I do.' You know what those coins would be worth today?"

"For richer, for poorer," Jackson reminded him. "And you still have the gold."

"Half of it. And it wouldn't exactly go over too well if I hawked the ring, would it?"

So *that* was the reason behind his dislike of gold all those years. But still there was a glaring deficiency in his father's viewpoint that Jackson could not ignore. "But, Dad, the ring *is* a symbol. You can't put a dollar value on love."

"I know," he said limply.

It sounded awful. Like he didn't really care anymore. Like there were other, more important reasons their love had gone down as the price of gold had gone up.

Jackson sat there in a pained silence.

"We're staying right here," he said finally, "until Mom

comes."

"I have to go to work."

"No!" It was time to get aggressive. It was time for his father to experience snarly adolescent rebellion for the first time. "We're not moving from this house until she gets here. I'm taking matters into my own hands . . ."

"You don't understand. You're only a teenager."

It was the last straw.

"One more word and and I'll never so much as open my mouth in this house again!"

"Jackson!"

"And that includes eating!"

"I don't believe it."

"Believe it!"

He had wounded his father deeper than ever before. It was pitiful to see — the man fighting off a quivering in his upper lip, awkwardly trying to spoon the last of the cereal into his mouth. When he swallowed, it was obviously serving more than one purpose.

When his father eased himself off the chair and left the kitchen it was with the look of a deflated man. He needed space to recover. Jackson could only sit there like some midafternoon soap opera character and wait to see if his lies and threats were going to work. It was no fun playing the obnoxious son, but he knew it was either that or watch his family become a complete write-off.

They were an anxious several minutes, made even worse by his refusal to eat. It was going against his every natural instinct while in a kitchen. To take his mind off it, and in full confidence that his father was not going to go anywhere, he took out his mother's diary, which he had stuck inside the waistband of his jeans.

He opened it up to the last entry. He checked his pocket to make sure the pizza medal was there. Then he waited some more. Hunger was building up in all its early-morning intensity. His stomach groaned — a rallying cry! He would not give in.

Seconds later the doorbell rang. The door opened. "Jackson." His mother was entering her own house as though she was an intruder.

Jackson jumped up from the table and stood in the doorway. He called first to his father, wherever he was, and then to his mother.

"Both of you. In the kitchen. Now! Please." He would not forget his manners.

His mother showed up first. "Why has your father not gone to — "

"Mom, this is no time for the mundane."

Then she noticed the open book on the table. "That's my diary. That's private, Jackson. Where did you get it?"

He ignored the question. "Except for me there wouldn't be a diary. Except for me the day I was born wouldn't have been the happiest day of your lives. It probably woulda been that time you won the bus trip for two to Niagara Falls."

His father entered just at that moment. "Yes, Jackson, you're right. Nothing could replace what we felt that day."

Jackson and his mother exchanged glances. Neither of them had expected him to admit such a thing. Something had stirred in the man. The fire wasn't completely dead. Jackson knew he would have to act fast if it was going to be any more than another flicker.

"I want you both to sit down," Jackson said.

They hesitated.

"Now! Please."

Like good parents, they did as they were told.

He continued. "I know it's still a bit early in the morning for a new life experience, and I know what I'm going to ask you to do is not something you're going to fully understand, but believe me, it's all for your own good. You'll be thanking me for this when you're older. I've been through it all, I should know."

"But, Jackson — "

"No buts about it. This is harder on me than it is on you."

"I bet this is a new kind of therapy, like an adult version of Tough Love," his mother said. "I wonder if Oprah Winfrey knows about this."

Jackson smiled for a brief few seconds, thankful that what he was doing was finally gaining some credibility.

"Quickly," he said, "do as I say. This is all part of the procedure."

He made them each place one hand flat on the table as he had done. He laid the open diary on their hands and at an angle where they all could read it. The pizza medal he positioned on the blank page opposite the final entry. He laid it there with the crust side up in the hope he wouldn't have to explain what it was.

"Now rub this medal and read along with me."

They looked at Jackson with vacant, confused stares.

"Trust me."

It was a simple and honest plea from the one person they both cared about more than anyone else in the world. Jackson started to read aloud in a ceremoniously solemn voice. "We are both amazed that we have produced such a dear, sweet son. We're sure he'll grow up to be truly original."

He nodded to his father and mother. They looked at each other, then at the page, and continued together where he had left off. "John has made a fabulous meal for the two of us in celebration. It is the happiest day of our life together."

Jackson had closed his eyes in earnest prayer that their three lives together had the essential elements needed to make a great story, one that deserved to be edged in gold and bound in leather.

He opened them and a blissful smile spread across his face. His father and mother had ceased all movement, as if their minds had gone into suspension, awaiting treatment.

There was no time to glory in his accomplishment, for his body too was slowing to a stop. Faith could indeed work miracles. His eyes slowly closed again, leaving him with the distinct feeling that somewhere far away he was about to be reborn.

TWELVE

John and Katherine regained consciousness in Room 203 of the maternity section of the Grace Hospital in St. John's, Newfoundland. Jackson was nowhere to be seen.

Wonderful aromas drifted into John's nostrils. They alerted him to the fact that he was sharing a tray of food with his wife as she rested in a hospital bed and he sat next to her. The whole scene bewildered them both, more especially John, whose sense of smell had been so recently dependent on McDonald's for stimulation.

They looked at each other and then all about the room. Both sets of eyes stopped at a calendar on the wall.

"My God," he said. "I think we've gone back to the time Jackson was born."

"Déjà vu?" Katherine whispered apprehensively.

John shrugged his eyebrows. "Hypnosis?"

"Perhaps we've reached one of those new levels of consciousness."

"Maybe," he said, with what sounded like hope.

Katherine took a bread roll from the tray and examined it. "Whole wheat and onion, exactly the ones you used to make." She gazed at the rest of the food. She remembered it all.

"What will we do?" he wondered.

"Perhaps we should eat it. Maybe it's all part of the procedure Jackson was talking about."

John smiled cautiously. "I could really use a good meal."

They ate together, awkwardly at first, but then, as the meal started to bring back the flavor of good times shared long ago, a somewhat more relaxed atmosphere took hold.

"You slept for a while after the baby was born, remember, and I went home," John said after a mouthful of cod au gratin.

She paused, her fork in midair. "And you came back with all this food. You knew I didn't like hospital meals." She returned to her salad. "Your special dressing. I always liked that combination of garlic and cucumber."

"Salads were my specialty."

She looked away for a long time, hard in thought, it seemed. Finally she glanced his way again.

"I hate to say it, but you were a real artist when it came to food."

John's eyes took on a new intensity. "You never said that before."

"Dammit, John, didn't you realize how hard that was to admit when I was trying to be an artist myself?"

"Katherine, you did some wonderful work with twine and rope."

"Don't patronize me, John. Macramé is a dead art. Nobody takes it seriously anymore."

"You could revive it. Who ever thought that tie-dying would make a comeback?"

She sneered and looked away. "Thanks . . . but I don't think so."

John walked over to the window. He stared out for a long time before saying anything.

"I always did like this city. There's a real sense of history here. That smell of salt water . . . Look, I can see Signal Hill, where we were married."

She got up from the bed and went over to where he was

standing. Against her better judgment, she broke into a smile, remembering. She started to hum, then sing. He joined her on the chorus, "Come together, right now, over me . . ."

They looked at each other, thinking back, but knowing that it was a long, long time ago. There would be no embracing each other now. She returned to the food.

"A lot has happened since then," she said, bringing him back to a kind of reality.

She was right. It was no sense thinking they could recapture the fervor of their marriage ceremony. He was still a Virgo and she was still a Taurus, but that really didn't matter that much anymore.

"Why the hell did you want to leave Newfoundland so badly?" she said, dipping a strawberry in brown sugar and then yoghurt.

It caught him unaware. He thought for a moment. "I never ever told you this before," he began quietly. "I had this idea of opening a combination bake shop, salad bar and craft store."

"The market for macramé had peaked long before that."

"I know, I know. But I was optimistic. Until I went to the bank and looked into getting a loan. It was hopeless. And then the baby got older and started to talk and I was feeling the pressure. Besides, I was tired of living in a have-not province."

"I felt it too."

"And then when Toronto got its own baseball team and Reagan announced he was running for president, I just couldn't take any more. There was money to be made and here I was baking multi-grain bread for a natural food store on this rock of a place stuck out in the Atlantic."

"Still . . ."

He looked out the window again. "I know. It does feel like home."

She walked to the window and looked at the way the fog was swirling around Signal Hill. "You're right, it does."

"Maybe things would have been different if we stayed."

"You mean . . . us?" she asked.

"It's possible."

She hesitated. She didn't want him to think for a second she was giving in.

"Something happened to you, John, after we went away. You lost your perspective. Getting into the microwave business somehow did strange things to your mind. You left Newfoundland and you lost sight of something very important things. Faster is not always better, John. Sometimes you have to put that computer aside and work things out in your head."

She had said the same thing before, of course, in other ways, at other times. But now, standing as they were at the window, the fog having completely obscured the hill where they were married, he was not dismissing it in the way he used to.

For one thing, he was stammering. "It wasn't only me. You loved getting a suntan in May instead of watching icebergs like we used to. You loved the fact that you weren't expected to like seal flipper pie. You said so yourself."

"I was trying to look on the bright side, John. I was looking for compensations."

He stood for a long time, staring at her.

"Change won't come easy," he said finally.

"The tougher the fight, the sweeter the prize."

He smiled. "That's what you said when you went into labor. I still remember your look of determination through all that pain."

"It was a wonderful moment when he was finally born," she said.

"It was the happiest day of our life together."

And then he, too, smiled and put his arms around her and kissed her, as tenderly as he had that same day sixteen years before.

The kiss ended only when a noise in the hallway became too loud for them to ignore. They turned together and stared at the door as through it burst a nurse out of breath and stricken with fright.

The nurse was stopped momentarily in her tracks. "You cut

your hair," she said to Katherine. "And you shaved your beard," she said to John. "It makes you both look . . . older." She shook her head as if to regain her senses.

"Calm down," John said. "It's not that bad."

"No, no, " she said. "Come with me. Hurry!"

They followed her out the door and down the hall.

"Something terrible has happened!"

"What? What?"

They could barely keep up with her, she had set such a pace.

"Look!" she said, coming to a sudden halt in front of the viewing window of the nursery.

John and Katherine stared in amazement. In the nursery, among all the newborns bundled in pink and blue blankets inside their little Plexiglas cribs, was a hulk of a teenager! All that could fit of him, too, was in one of the cribs. The rest — head, arms, legs, and size 11 basketball-sneakered feet — was hanging over the sides. He wasn't moving. Like all the others, he was sound asleep.

"It's Jackson!" Katherine blurted out.

"It's our son," John said to the nurse in an unsuccessful attempt to control her hysteria.

The commotion brought a rush of nurses, aides and orderlies to the nursery window. They made such a racket that it woke one of the babies. Her pink blanket began to quiver and soon she started to howl. Within seconds another joined in, and then another, and soon poor Jackson was surrounded by a dozen screeching infants. It could have made a great ad for Planned Parenthood.

By the time Jackson was awake enough to realize where he had ended up, his father and mother and a mob of hospital staff had donned surgical masks and were surrounding him, demanding answers. What followed was a bewildering combination of newborn wailing, muffled adult ranting and a lone adolescent voice of reason.

"Perhaps I was born with a very active pituitary gland," Jackson yelled at them. He sprang from the Plexiglas and took off out of the room.

John and Katherine ran to catch up, the others tight behind them. His parents rushed Jackson to the door of their room and the three of them dashed inside. Jackson threw all his weight against the door to hold off the mass of uniformed people trying to get in.

"What are we going to do?!" his mother shouted frantically.

"Renew your marriage vows," Jackson told them.

"What?"

"Renew your marriage vows!"

His parents looked at each other, then at the calendar, and then at Jackson.

"Quick, join hands!" Jackson said, urging them on. "It's our only hope. I can't hold them off much longer." He dug the pizza medal out of his pocket.

John held out his left hand, his ring shining brighter than it had in years.

With all the drama of slow motion, Katherine did the same. She placed her hand in his.

Jackson clasped his hand that held the medal over them both. "I'll start you off." He took a deep breath and, in the most reverential voice he could muster under the circumstances, he began, "To have and to hold . . ."

And with the three of them together helping each other with the words, they continued, "From this day forward, for better for worse, for richer for poorer, in sickness and in health, to love and to cherish . . ."

Thus joined together, their voices began a slow, timeless fade, then fell silent. Their bodies, too, quietly passed away.

Jackson's hold on the door was no longer an impediment, and through it the hospital staff fell together in a white heap. But even with all that weight there was nothing left that they could ever put asunder.

THIRTEEN

Jackson and his parents checked each other over from across the kitchen table. They all looked like they should have been out of breath. Jackson glanced at his watch. It had been a very demanding few minutes.

He closed the diary and slipped it out of sight. As he did so the pizza medal dropped with a clatter to the table, startling his parents into realizing they were back to the world as they had known it.

But their world was not at all the same one they had left. That was quickly apparent from the way his father slipped his hand into Katherine's.

"Kath," he said, "I guess we really need to talk."

She didn't know what to say, and she took so long trying to come up with it that Jackson decided he better say it for her. "I bet we all could use something to eat."

His father turned to him. "You go ahead, whatever you want. Bacon and eggs? French toast and syrup? Sugar Crisps? . . . Just kidding on the Sugar Crisps."

For a second Jackson thought the trip might have done his father permanent damage. He settled for a quick cup of coffee.

"I'll have one too," his mother said. "I really need something to wake me up."

His father smiled. "Make that three."

"It's not decaffeinated," Jackson told him.

His father hesitated, then said, "What the hell. You can't play it safe all the time, right?"

Was he kidding? The trip was obviously producing side effects Jackson hadn't counted on. He was hardly prepared for a father who dealt with stress in this way.

Jackson's head was still reeling from the last comment when his father loosened his tie, undid his top button and said, "Jackson, I've been thinking. Maybe we should take up some new sport together. Golf? Would you like to try golf? . . . No? Squash? Maybe that's something more our speed."

Jackson struggled for words. "Maybe," he managed to get out finally, "I better get to school."

He gave them both a quick good-bye and hurried down the hall and out the front door. He immediately drew in a massive breath of fresh air.

He had done all he could do. They were on their own now. He walked away from the house, finding it hard to imagine just what his parents might be going through inside.

The walk to school was, thankfully, a long one. Usually he got a ride or took the bus, but this morning he needed the extra time alone to unwind and readjust to normal, everyday life.

He found himself looking at the world around him with a more innocent, child-like perspective. He was rediscovering just how badly the streets were jammed with early-morning traffic and just how many flashing signs there were to make people aware of things they didn't want to find out. It was his world, the one he knew best. But he was feeling less comfortable here now, less a part of the crowd.

He stopped along the way at a drugstore and bought a drinking box of a vitamin-enriched blend of citrus juices. He tried to savor the tastiness and nutrition the ads had told him was to be found there, without much success. He found himself holding onto the empty box, feeling guilty that in a hundred years the box might still be around to remind someone of his thirst for convenience. With every step he was sensing the need for greener grass and more open spaces.

He approached the school with a greater sense of himself than ever before. He headed for his homeroom, feeling like a new man.

The first people he saw outside the door were Sara and Adam. Sara was holding something in her hand. As he walked closer, Jackson could see the minute bit of the gold chain not covered by her fingers. She was handing the chain back to Adam with words that Jackson would have overheard anyway, regardless if he had been straining his ears.

He said nothing to them, but turned and went into the classroom. He was finding it impossible to keep from smiling knowingly to himself.

After a few minutes Sara came in, followed by what Jackson hoped was her ex-boyfriend. Sara cast Jackson a glance. He could see she was restraining herself, out of respect for the guy. Jackson held back, too. He was not one to gloat, although there was no denying his feelings that he was infinitely more suited to her than Adam had ever been.

The rest of the morning was a tremendous strain on his powers of concentration. Trigonometry and The Wars of the Roses seemed less relevant than usual, and even the discussion of several dreaded diseases in biology class didn't hold much interest for him.

By lunchtime he was starving for the chance to sit down with Sara in the cafeteria. He found her in a corner table by herself. He slipped into the seat next to her. Over a pork cutlet, french fries and a pastry with an unrecognizable filling, the words just flowed from him, words that on the surface might not have seemed very profound, but through which ran everything he felt for her, and would always feel, no matter how their lives changed, or what obstacles were thrown in his way, or just how true it was what scientists were predicting about the earth.

"Jackson, slow down, you're not chewing your food properly," she said, seriously at first, but then with a smile.

He loved that bit of a mother in her.

"Know something?"

"What?" she said.

"You're the best thing that ever happened to me. I could live on love, I really could."

"Sure," she said, teasing of course.

She laughed then. She looked into his eyes. "It was a hard choice. But I decided I had to give it a try."

And that was another thing he loved about her — her honesty. "You won't be sorry," he said.

It was a hint of the conversations he had dreamed of having — lighthearted, playful, full of the give-and-take that let each of them be their own person. He was sure theirs would be a really modern relationship, with none of that petty jealousy that he had seen come between so many other couples when they first started going with each other.

As he continued to eat he tried to decide whether he should bring up the whole business about his parents. By the time he was through the dessert he had decided against it. It might just turn out to be too much of a headache to inflict on anyone so early in a relationship. He didn't want anything to take away from those first few glorious, heart-swirling days of getting to know each other better.

There was a sense of calm, a quiet after the stormy struggle to win her. They lingered over each other at the table. Jackson let his mind soak in the unspeakable magic of being in love. He didn't want it to end.

"We should go," she said, so quietly as not to break the spell entirely. They were the only ones left in the cafeteria.

"We should," he said. But they didn't until the buzzer signaling five minutes to class roused them and sent him stumbling back to being a listless student again.

It was Sara who warned him of what he was doing to himself. In the middle of French class she looked across at him and mouthed the words with an intenseness that even he found alarming. "Jackson," she mouthed, "snap out of it!" He thought she was conjugating a particularly irregular verb.

After class she explained herself more fully. "Jackson, you're going to blow it. Can't you see what you're doing?"

"What do you mean?"

"What I mean is you're so far behind in your courses that if you don't do some work, you're going to fail. You've got to get your mind back on school before it's too late."

"Right."

"Who do you think'll have the last laugh if you don't?"

It took the image of Adam sporting a smug little grin to make Jackson face up to his situation. He had a hellishly long list of assignments to do. And then he had lab reports to write, and reports to give on books he hadn't even started yet. And exams.

Undaunted by his list, Sara offered to help. He had expected an extraordinary relationship, but never in his wildest dreams did he think she might want to guide him through the maze of schoolwork that he somehow had to get done.

They met after school and planned their strategy. She volunteered to come over to his place every night for two hours to help him get down to work. Sounded very good to him.

There was one problem. He didn't bring it up for fear of appearing reluctant. There might not be a home for her to come to if his father and mother hadn't worked things out.

When they left the classroom and went to their lockers (after a wet kiss by the same water fountain where he had first expressed his true feelings for her), he still hadn't mentioned it. Outside the school, they walked hand-in-hand and laughed together and he said crazy things to her as if he hadn't a care in the world. He wasn't about to risk messing things up by bringing his family into it.

He walked her home. He didn't want it to end, but he knew there would be many more times that would be just as fantastic. By the time they parted he was so struck with her that he had a whole new appreciation of puberty. His walk could not contain the feelings that were erupting throughout his body. He ran and jumped and from time to time made wildly excited noises all the way home.

He had no idea what to expect when he went inside the house. Both cars were in the driveway, which made no sense to him. His father had never come home from work early except for the day in the middle of the last recession when an irate stock holder had threatened to blow himself up in the company's newly renovated offices.

It turned out that his father had not even gone to work. Jackson was truly amazed.

"I called in sick," his father said. He even winked at him. Jackson knew his most bizarre dreams could never have produced this image of his father coming down the stairs with an arm tight around his mother's waist.

"Me, too," his mother added. It was not something Jackson could ever have prepared himself for. He stood there, his mouth open.

And as if that wasn't enough for his stunned adolescent mind, out came his mother with another wallop.

"Jackson, your father and I have been trying to make up our minds about something and we want your opinion." That in itself was enough to send him groping for something to lean against. "Since this morning we've had this intense urge to have another child . . . together."

Uncontrolled neurons swept through Jackson's brain, forcing their way down paths that had never been used before. He shut his eyes to block out the added confusion of his parents grinning at each other, but when he opened them again he still couldn't get a word out. He could barely keep his knees from buckling under him.

"Wouldn't you like a baby brother?" his mother said.

"Or sister, Kath," his father said.

"Or both," they said together. They laughed at how similarly their minds were working.

Oh, God, please! If there was ever a time in his life he wanted to call upon God for answers to the great mysteries of the universe, it was now. He wasn't looking for much, just enough to get him through the little remaining time he had to live at home with his parents.

"No hurry, Jackson. You think about it." They walked past him, smiling at each other for reasons that Jackson had no interest whatsoever in understanding.

"Let's make dinner, together," they said . . . together.

Jackson raced up to his bedroom. He locked the door behind him and leaned against it just like people did in movies when they were trying to escape from unknown beings. He checked his room to make sure he hadn't been caught in some grotesque warp of his imagination. The room looked normal enough. The bed, the battered skateboard, the poster of Gauguin's girls on the wall — they all stirred up the same unrealistic longings as before. Nothing had changed.

He was forced to conclude that the display by his parents on the staircase had indeed been the real thing. What had gone on between them while he was asleep in the hospital, he had no idea, but it seemed the two had managed to put life back into something that had been dying for years. For that Jackson should have been able to breathe easier. After all, he had risked a lot to see it happen. But instead his head was clogged with the notion that none of it made good sense, that they weren't acting like real parents, that what he had done was cause them to revert to being the flower children they were when they first met.

What made the least sense to him was all the talk of having another child. If they wanted new life in their marriage, why didn't they think about a Shih Tzu or a Shar-pei. He knew it was looking odder and odder to be forty and not be out pushing a stroller, but that was no reason to bring a poor, sweet, innocent child into their world.

He was being unfair. In a couple of years he would be gone. They would need something to take their minds off what a college education was costing them. It was just that he could see in the meantime all their time and energy and money being taken up with this new kid, turning Jackson into a neglected and resentful older brother. They would be sorry they ever conceived so much as the idea of a child.

Now he was being grossly unfair. He was overreacting. He had to cool it. He put his mind where it should have been — on his schoolwork. It cooled rapidly, but he was left feeling exceedingly melancholy. He found no comfort in the fact that the assignment he had to work on was about hazardous-waste disposal.

He had just managed to immerse himself in the opening paragraph when he heard a call for dinner. He had no choice but to trudge down to the kitchen, his teeth gritting in anticipation of whatever little surprises the two of them had cooked up.

"We've been thinking," his mother said, pausing to fill his wineglass.

Jackson braced himself.

"We've been thinking that maybe we should all move . . . back to Newfoundland."

"Ever hear of hydroponics?" his father cut in. "I saw an ad in the newspaper. There's a company there looking for someone to develop a new strategy for marketing cucumbers."

The wine going down Jackson's throat had long ago decided to change direction, but Jackson swallowed hard and kept it under control.

"I know, I know, it's all a bit of a surprise. So what we've decided is that we all should have time away to think about it. How does a weekend in New York sound to you? There's a flight out in a few hours."

Jackson was not quite so successful with his second mouthful of wine. It came sputtering out and into his napkin.

"Sorry," he croaked.

"There's more," said his father.

Jackson had hardly made it through the first announcements

with his nervous system intact. He steadied himself with his hands on the edge of the table.

"You get to choose the restaurants and you get to order whatever you want."

They beamed like such a pair of kind and thoughtful parents when they said it, that he hardly knew what to do. He should have been delighted, and if he gave way to his gut feelings, he would have been. But somehow the idea of spending a weekend in New York with the two of them in their present state was far from an attractive propostion.

"Why don't you two go alone? Sort of like a second honeymoon," he suggested, trying not to sound ungrateful.

"What, and leave you here when you had your heart set on going back? Not on your life."

"I have too much schoolwork, I can't go. I need every spare moment to catch up." It was all he could do to keep from sounding like he was pleading.

"You'd go crazy by yourself in this big house all weekend."

"Trust me, I won't go crazy."

His parents looked at each other for an embarrassingly long time, and then they looked at Jackson in a way that suggested that they just might be persuaded.

"Leave lots for me to eat," Jackson added quickly, "and then you can go with a clear conscience."

"How about enough money so you can eat out all weekend?"

"Mmmmmmmm!"

His enthusiasm seemed to rid his parents of that last bit of guilt.

He dug into the alfalfa sprouts and their bed of lettuce with a zest that left his parents marveling more than ever at his appetite. He purred his way through the fish that followed, then finished the meal with an endless string of compliments for the yoghurt fruit cup that was for dessert. He left the table with his parents soundly convinced that a weekend of unrestricted eating would be as exciting for him as a weekend roaming the streets of New York.

He returned to his bedroom and to the solace of his hazardous-waste assignment. He set his mind firmly on writing the paper.

In the midst of a particularly strong sentence about the world as we know it being rather screwed up, a knock came on his door. It was his mother. She said she wanted to talk to him. He struggled to answer the door with complete calm, as if she were the very same mother he had cherished all these sixteen years, in the same way that she did him, her only child.

"What the hell's happened to him?" Jackson exploded before she got a word out.

"Well . . ."

"Mom, for heaven's sakes!" It was not a time when patience seemed much of a virtue.

"Jackson, I'm not entirely sure. But it's wonderful. You know what he wants to buy in New York? A compact disc player. He's a new man."

"Mom, Mom . . ."

"I know, I know. But it's more than that," she said slowly. "He seems to care about me, Jackson, in a way that he hasn't cared about me in a long, long time."

It was a tender moment and he hardly wanted to spoil it, but he was determined to be practical about the whole thing.

"Mom, really."

"I know it's hard to believe. But I've just spent a whole day with him. Nobody could put on an act like that for a whole day. The man has definitely changed. There's no other explanation."

"But — "

"I realize it's a shock. But isn't it wonderful!"

"All that talk about a baby . . ."

"It's crazy, I know, but isn't it wonderful."

The woman had obviously fallen in love all over again. There was no other way he could account for such an upset in the normal, rational functioning of her mind. And there would be no way to talk sense to her. He would just have to let it run its course and pray to God that she didn't get pregnant. Parents nowadays! Aren't they old enough to have better sense? What, he asked himself, was the world coming to?

His father knocked on the door and came into the room, timidly at first, but then looking terribly pleased with himself for having the nerve to wear what he was wearing — cream-colored pants and a pastel blue-green cotton sweater and a sports jacket that was anything but a Harris Tweed.

"Like it?" he said, somewhat buoyantly.

"Amazing," Jackson said. "Really."

"We better get going, Kath, or we'll miss our flight."

Jackson was still looking amazed when they went out the door and gathered up their luggage. In a few minutes he was following them down the stairs.

His mother listed off a steady stream of things not to forget to do while they were gone. Jackson found it slightly reassuring. Perhaps she was the same mother after all.

"Behave yourself, now," she said, her final words as she went out the door.

"You, too."

When they had put the luggage in the car and his mother was inside with her seatbelt on, Jackson called his father aside and put one hand firmly on his shoulder. He slipped his trio of condoms into his father's hand.

"Better safe than sorry," Jackson said. "Don't do anything you'll live to regret."

His father smiled shyly. "Son . . . ," he started, but his voice trailed off. Jackson winked at him.

And then they drove away and Jackson was left standing alone in the driveway. His hand was still in the air, waving slightly, well after the car was out of sight. He walked slowly back to the house. It was a moment as touching as any in the TV commercials for phoning long distance.

He kicked about the house for a while, feeling good that at least it was still his home. He toyed with several ideas on how to use what few spare moments he would have between working and eating and having a good time with Sara.

He was drawn against his better judgment into the living room and to the bookshelf. He stared at his father's collection. They were no longer neatly lined in rigid rows. They stuck out and leaned against each other, and there was even one on its side, as if someone had been reading it and had casually put it down to return to later. It made his heart swell to see such disorder.

It was this stirring in his blood that sent his mind to wondering if he didn't deserve a little reward for all the pain some of these books had caused him. It was almost embarrassing to think about, but he was kinda thinking that he wouldn't sorta mind being a bit more experienced as far as some of his . . . natural desires were concerned.

He took down *Lady Chatterley's Lover* and sat in the armchair with it. He started wandering through page by page, a little uneasy about what he might find. Perhaps he wouldn't be up to what might be expected of him. He knew it was only natural to feel that way his first time and all, but still he could feel himself getting sweaty.

He shut the book and took a few deep breaths. He gathered his courage and reached slowly into his pocket and took out the pizza medal. For a while he let it rest there in the palm of his hand.

His eyes shifted from the medal to the book and back again. An all-expense-paid return trip for one. The holiday of your dreams. Experience of a lifetime.

Too good to pass up.

He shoved the medal back into his pocket and whipped open the book again. His breathing started to get heavy.

Gold. He was forgetting the other piece of gold. He'd take a chance. Her jewelry, she was wealthy, there was sure to be some somewhere.

The doorbell rang.

He shut the book. Damn! Damn! And then he took several

deep breaths to try to calm himself. He put the book back on the shelf. The doorbell rang again. He pulled his oversized sweatshirt down as far as he could to cover his enthusiasm.

He opened the door.

"All ready?" Sara asked.

"We said seven."

She checked her watch. "It is seven. Must be your watch."

He looked at his Rolex as he closed the door behind her. She was right. It had died an untimely death. He took it off and whacked it against his open hand. He did it again and again. Still nothing moved. He was both frustrated and embarrassed.

"Have you had anything to eat yet?" she asked.

She sure knew how to comfort a guy. He nodded. "But we'll order in anyway. Pizza? Chicken? Chinese?"

"You decide."

He could feel his heart opening up to her even more. "Pizza, with pepperoni, mushrooms, onions, green pepper, bacon and double cheese," he said, loving every word.

She smiled. He did too, and went to the phone and called in the order to Masterpizza.

Later, she followed him upstairs to his room. She looked around, her eyes eventually stopping at his Gauguin poster. lll"I love Gauguin, don't you?" he said. "I find his nudes so . . . so . . . "

"Compatible?"

He knew the poster would have to go.

Then suddenly it struck him — he might be going too, moving away, if his father and mother had their way. It was altogether too heart-breaking to think that the girl he had worked so hard to win might be gone from his life even more quickly than she had come into it.

"Ever go back to Newfoundland?" he asked mournfully.

"Every summer, to visit my grandparents. Actually I'm thinking about going to university there."

"Whoa!"

When the doorbell rang, he was still picturing them snug together on a beach as the broad Atlantic lapped the shore.

She reminded him about the pizza. He fumbled in his pockets for money to pay for it.

As soon as she left the room he went straight for the poster. He hated to see it go, but he could understand her feelings. He carefully removed the tacks. He spread the poster out on his bed, rolled it up and found a place for it in his closet, close to where he used to hide the . . .

He raced out the door. "The pizza medal!"

He met her at the head of the stairs. "Is this what you're looking for?" she said, handing the pizza medal to him. "The woman who's delivering the pizza . . . She told me how you got it."

Jackson looked past her down the stairs. He could see Mrs. Landsberg standing in the doorway. He ran down to her.

"Hi, Jackson." She wasn't the chirpy ex-librarian she had been a few days before.

"Mrs. Landsberg, you deliver the pizza, too?"

"I had to. It's the only order we've had all evening."

"Really."

"It's just not working out, Jackson."

"You mean you're going to have to close the place?"

"I think I might have turned customers off when I got mad at them for getting tomato sauce on the books. I never knew people could be such messy readers."

"But you started off with such a bang."

"Too big a bang, I guess."

Jackson opened his hand and stared at the pizza medal.

"You want it back?" he asked. "To help pay the bills?"

"You won it, Jackson. It's yours."

Did he really want to keep it? Did he really need it anymore? Hadn't it brought him the girl of his dreams and a family that loved one another more than ever? What more could he possibly want?

"Tell you what," he said. "I'll trade you for the pizza."

She hesitated, still no businesswoman. "I couldn't do that."

He took the pizza and put the medal into her hand.

She hugged him, finding it hard to adequately express her thankfulness. "Too mucha for words," she offered weakly.

"See you back at the library?"

She smiled and shrugged. "You're so . . . so sweet, Jackson. If I was forty years younger . . . "

He was still forcing out laughter as she walked to her car.

He went slowly back up the stairs. He wondered if he had done right by not telling her what amazing things the medal could do. It might make for a whole different story.

He found Sara in his room, sitting on his bed, staring at a blank wall. He sat down next to her with the pizza. He flipped up the lid, then turned to her and smiled.

She looked at him, smiled and shook her head. She took the first slice.

He felt himself a man ready to savor the timeless, priceless pleasures of this life — love and a good meal. He had no desire whatsoever to be anywhere else in the entire world, not even New York.

Other books by Kevin Major:

Blood Red Ochre

Attracted to Nancy's mysterious behavior and "foreign"
looks, David is glad to work with her on a history assignment
concerning the Beothuk Indians. But when they journey to Red
Ochre Island, a burial place for the Beothuk, past and present
merge together as Dauoodaset, the last of the Beothuk, tells of
the final desperate days of his people in a gripping parallel
narrative.   176p

Doubleday hardcover $15.95   ISBN 0-385-29794-7

Dear Bruce Springsteen

"Having no one else to confide in, Terry, 14, writes to 'The Boss,' knowing he'll probably never receive a response.... Major understands well the inner workings of teenagers and expresses, in an authentic voice, the turmoil and sorting out processes that go along with growing up.... Eloquent, penetrating." – *Publishers Weekly*   144p

Doubleday hardcover $14.95   ISBN 0-385-29584-7
A Dell Laurel-Leaf Paperback $3.95 0-440-20410-0

Far From Shore

Arrested for a crime he can't remember committing, a 15-year-old Christopher must learn to make a life of his own in a family torn apart by unemployment, alcoholism, and a young man's rebellious needs. "Captivating. Major has written the story from several points of view, giving true insight into human behavior and motivation." – *Children's Book Review Service*

224p

"As good a YA novel as there is around." – *ALAN Review.*

A School Library Journal Best Book of the Year, Canadian Young Adult Book Award.

A Dell Laurel-Leaf Paperback $3.95   ISBN 0-440-92585-1

Hold Fast

Two runaway cousins, Michael and Curtis, struggle to survive without money, family or friends as they wander through the harsh, magnificent landscape of Newfoundland. "A classic innocent who sometimes sounds like a sort of Newfoundland Holden Caulfield, Michael is more than redeemed as a character by the directness and strength of his emotions." – *Kirkus Reviews*   224p

A School Library Journal Best Book of the Year

The Canada Council Children's Literature Award

Association of Canadian Libraries Book of the Year

Hans Christian Honor List

A Dell Laurel-Leaf Paperback $3.95   ISBN 0-440-93756-6

Thirty-six Exposures

As the end of high school nears, quiet Lorne finds his camera no longer a shield but an instrument forcing him to focus on events that seem to be racing out of control in his small Newfoundland town. "A compelling coming-of-age novel with a message." – *Booklist*   160p

"Probably the best Canadian portrait ever drawn of seventeen-going-on-adult." – *Atlantic Insight*

A Dell Laurel-Leaf Paperback $3.95 ISBN 0-440-20163-2